STRANGERS IN PARIS

"It was wonderful to arrive in Paris by night. A drizzling rain was falling and it gave the streets an exciting mystery. The shops were brightly lit. The pavement was multidinous with umbrellas and the water dripping on them glistened dimly under the street lamps . . . Sometimes a gust of wind made women crouch under their umbrellas and their skirts swirled round their legs."

—*Stranger in Paris* by W. Somerset Maugham

STRANGERS IN PARIS

New Writing
Inspired by the City of Light

Edited by Megan Fernandes & David Barnes

Tightrope Books

Tightrope Books   Copyedited by Shirarose Wilensky & Alanna Lipson.
17 Greyton Crescent   Cover design by Karen Correia Da Silva.
Toronto, Ontario   Text design by Shirarose Wilensky.
M6E 2G1 Canada
www.TightropeBooks.com

Printed in Canada.

"Le Passeur/The Guide Across Frontiers," by John Berger is an extract from *Here Is Where We Meet* (Bloomsbury, London, 2005; Pantheon, NY, 2005), reprinted with permission from the publisher.

"It is not enough that the buds have come out . . .," "Here we are on the Place Saint-Sulpice again . . .," and "The well-tempered clavicle" by Eleni Sikelianos from *Earliest Worlds* (Coffee House Press, 2001) are reprinted with permission from the publisher.

"Straining" (*Flying Inland*, Doubleday, 1973), and "Pale Light in the Luxembourg Garden" and "Monet's Path" (*A History of Yearning*, The Sow's Ear, 2009) by Kathleen Spivack are reprinted with permission from the respective publishers.

LIBRARY AND ARCHIVES CANADA CATALOGUING IN PUBLICATION

Strangers in Paris: new writing inspired by the city of light / edited by Megan Fernandes & David Barnes.

ISBN 978-1-926639-32-1

1. Paris (France)—Literary collections. 2. English literature—21st century. 3. American literature—21st century. 4. Canadian literature (English)—21st century. I. Fernandes, Megan, 1985– II. Barnes, David, 1971–

PR1111.P37S77 2011   820.8'03244361   C2010-907707-5

Acknowledgements

The editors would like to thank Tightrope Books, especially Halli Villegas, Myna Wallin, and Shirarose Wilensky for their patience, support, and commitment to this project. We cannot overstate how lucky we feel to be working with such an astute and intuitive team of people. We are also enormously indebted to both Mia Bailey and Jonathan Hamrick for their tireless work and invaluable feedback during the editing process. Special thanks to Alice Notley, John Berger, Sarah Riggs, Jen K. Dick, Kathleen Spivack, Joshua Neves, the Spoken Word community in Belleville, and Sylvia Whitman and the staff at Shakespeare and Company for their support and guidance. And finally, thank you to Helen, Bruce, Albert, Isabel, Peter, Chris, Ida, James, and Alberto for many late nights of food and storytelling, without which these words and experiences would not be possible.

Sadly, we learned shortly before going to press that Jessica Malcomson, who contributed a story to this book, died early this year. She was a promising writer and a friend. We would like to dedicate this anthology to her memory.

TABLE OF CONTENTS

Contents

Contents

Contents

INTRODUCTIONS

Megan Fernandes
Poetry Editor

Sharifa came to Paris to write about Harlem. Sharifa is a young African-American woman from Houston, Texas, and the daughter of a professor and a visual artist. After an education at Harvard, she spent time living in New York, writing for the *New York Times Book Review*, reading literature, and exploring the craft of letterpress and book art. She liked to touch things and had a curious, rather old-fashioned interest in material culture; she would often press her fingers over the type of old books to assess the quality of the raise. She had an appreciation of craft, and I an appreciation for people who appreciated craft, since I myself had no patience for objects, only people.

In 2002 Sharifa moved to Harlem. She searched for an apartment near the old library, bought silk stockings and an old desk to outfit her new adventure in this neighbourhood. That's how Sharifa came to me in Paris: talking of Harlem, of an essay she wrote about Lenox Terminal, of a book deal with a major publisher, about Harlem and her spectres, her intersections, her reputation. Harlem and the endless relationships she had to black history, to NYC, to academia. "My book is about arrivals," she once told me while making soup, slicing carrots in neat orange circles. "Since I was fourteen I had a whole bookshelf of arrivals. Toomer, Hughes, McKay, all of them writing about getting to a place. The past comes through, of course, in the furniture, in new lovers who look like old ones, in the weather. The past gets told, but you can't start with that. We are not starting with stories of the past." I sat on her bed listening, falling in love with her, as I do with all my friends. Of all the world, here she sat as a collection of forces mapped by the neat coordinates of her Paris apartment across from the Gare de l'Est. Of all the world, she was here, sitting with me, making soup, talking of Harlem.

I find my encounter with Sharifa a compelling starting point for this anthology. Perhaps this is because, though she is not included in this collection, Sharifa is an example of how the modern writer in Paris has become mythologized in my mind. Paris, it seems, is the perfect model for the dilemma of how to weave the old and new, struggling with the tension between the city's historical voices and its status as a contemporary metropolis. Paris animates corners and conversations, dramatizes all the elements of urban living in order to make adventures, romances, and memoirs out of everything, and there is something both dark and philosophical about this compulsive storytelling impulse. "The French are anthropologists," the celebrated poet, Alice Notley, told me in our interview, "They think everything is poetry."

Paris is exhaustively committed to the word, to language, and the way it is treated as property, as a kind of cultural capital. In fact, Paris exists in an imaginary realm; she is obsessively preserving herself and, as outsiders, we want to consume her, to consume Frenchness in little epiphanic discoveries of stereotypes we already know too well—bread, wine, café life, high art. The city relies on narrative and, for this reason, it is difficult to take three steps in most parts of this city in any kind of anonymity. However, between these "postcard" structures and spaces is a history of a poetic imagination unique to her. Paris allows a way to examine oneself as a writer, and to expand and shape one's voice and work through associating with a community of thinkers who meet on a regular basis. Put simply (and rather unromantically, I might add), Paris is a place of expectations and deadlines; it is a productive city to write in because one never writes in isolation. This, more than plaques scattered around the city identifying former Hemingway residences, makes Paris most convincing as a writer's city. As the poetry editor for this collection, I have witnessed the illuminating results of a tight writers' community. For example, some of the shared aesthetic impulses include a mining for a strange new imagery, a fragmenting and careful reframing of the line, an experimenting in prose poems and micro-fictions, a fierce commitment to ekphrastic poetry, performance, translation, and a bilingual poetic sensibility.

More than just the city of Paris as the unifying thread for the voices included here, the poetry in this anthology has a palpable sense of urgency. This was neither expected nor solicited, but it seems that most of the poems are outbursts and possess real explosive energy, even when they appear meditative. These outbursts are not the joyful whims of Parisian discoveries as suggested earlier; on the contrary, these seem to be poets at a loss in confronting their environment, relationships, identity politics, and the routine of their everyday lives, both in Paris and at home. Rufo Quintavalle's short verse, rich in precise imagery of the city, is also moody, dark, and clutches at the reader, as if bemoaning something just beyond reach ("the sense of edges"). Alice Notley shares her blunt poetics of interrogation, a conversational style that is alert, direct, and even aggressive. "I want to be paid for my emotions, don't you?" Even Jorie Graham's poetry, haunting in its sound and dissociative imagery, is paced and lineated so that it builds, but builds toward the undoing of meaning and the subject, until some hard relief is granted to the reader: "the holy place shuts, baggy with evening, and here it is / finally night / bursting open / with hunt."

Suzanne Allen's ekphrastic poetry, in particular "An Hour with Madame Sabatier," which brings to life Auguste Clésigner's *Femme piquée par un serpent*, has one of the most memorable voices in the collection. She is hyper-attentive to her surroundings, but the speaker is also apologetically self-conscious of her participation in the scenes she creates, which are both playful and serious. There are also the delicate meditations of Sarah Riggs, who in her letter to Virginia Woolf, wavers between a plea and a wonderfully compelling sense of confused indebtedness: "I thought of you as I was getting out of the bath . . . I thought of horizontality . . . I am glad you left a note for Leonard." Another passage that particularly stands out is by the speaker of Judith Chriqui's "Holiday" in a confrontation with her French-Moroccan father about her panic attacks and self-medication, a prose poem detailing the humiliation of cross-generational cultural gaps. She begins in Tel Aviv: "You weren't there the following morning, the morning I awoke feeling strange." Most pieces document "encounters"; there is an *encountering* presence, which often manifests in a chilling stasis between the speaker and some absent figure, sometimes in the physical city, but also around the world with the imaginary realm of Paris never too far away. There is a way in which Paris can digress and travel like consciousness, a way in which she can be gathered far from herself into a "state of mind" or sprawl into seemingly unrelated memories. These are poems of "address," but they seem to address in every direction.

Perhaps this is why I hesitate to call this "expatriate writing," as I am uncertain of what "expatriatism" really means in our current state of globalization, which includes the internationalization of educational systems, EU citizenship, and the easy mobility of students and artists through ESL teaching, residencies, and fellowship programs. This anthology has no interest in reviving the myth of literary Paris or giving homage to those writers who came here to write in the twenties and thirties. As Hemingway said, he was tired of these "dirty, easy labels." Still, the history of literary Paris has resonance beyond its romanticization. It has become more complicated not only in addressing the identity politics of non-French men and women writing here, but also demands a re-evaluation of how our ideas and stereotypes about French culture circulate. Perhaps I felt this most strongly when I briefly worked in a high school in Clichy-sous-Bois, a suburb of Paris made infamous for the 2005 race riots. When I asked my students where they wanted to live when they grew up, they chatted happily about London, New York City, different parts of California, or returning to their parents' home countries of Tunisia, Morocco, Algeria, and Turkey. When I asked them about France, about staying in Paris, they responded with a kind of haughty laughter: "But we are not French." What then is at stake when writers come to write in France to *record* Frenchness and French experience? As Michael Kimmelman suggested in his April 2010 article in *The New York Times* on the future of the French Language: "What does French culture signify these days when there are some 200 million French speakers in the world but only 65 million are actually French? Culture in general—and not just French culture—has become increasingly unfixed, unstable, fragmentary and elective."[1]

For this reason among many, Paris seems to be a space of confrontation, not escape. There is a way in which Sharifa's Harlem seeped into my own writing. The same way my peers from Italy, from rural Ireland, from Norway provoke each other to confront not only their relationship with their different homelands, but also their fantasies of Paris, what they came to *gain* from Paris, and what it means to write here. How does Harlem, or the American South, or the Californian mountainscape find new articulation in the Tuileries gardens or the boulevards of Belleville? And this extends beyond easy comparisons of geography or cultural practices; "expat" writers in France are forced, in a very different way from writers in other cities, to justify, to explain, to subvert the cliché so much so that it becomes hackneyed to even talk about it. But today is a different Paris, and a very different *literary* Paris, which is hungry and desires a novel consideration regarding taste, language, and even citizenship. The word needs to be *replanted* in the city, and even though it may be rich with its historical voices, it needs to find new expression beyond its stereotypes. The city is much more than that. There are no words for what Paris *is*, perhaps, but it is more than its iconic representation.

I feel a great affection for the work presented here, and I will openly admit that this process has been very personal to my experience in Paris. This is for better or worse. This is the moment as I saw it, and the anthology includes writers who have been in Paris for more than twenty years and also those in the city for just a few months. "Strangers in Paris" is meant with some irony, but also seems to capture both the excitement and isolation of a temporary stay in an unknown city. Paris is not a casual city, and perhaps this is why the cinematic "Strangers" feels both parodic and sincere. For young writers especially, Paris is an easy city to make mistakes, to steal a good line, and with one ear listen to a reading by Susan Howe at the Centre Pompidou, and with the other ear, to be equally provoked by an un-

---

1   Kimmelman, Mark. "ABROAD; Pardon My French." *The New York Times*. April 25, 2010.

known voice at Spoken Word in Belleville. Because of this palimpsestic education, writers are able to hybridize their languages, aesthetics, and literary and cultural traditions into something that remains both authentic and meaningful. I hope this will engage the reader. More pointedly, these poems deserve to be in the company of one another, for whether intentional or not, they have helped produce and orchestrate each other's voices into a relentless and energetic conversation.

David Barnes
Prose Editor

Why write? Why come to Paris to write? Like the young Paul Auster, living in a tiny maid's room and—at that time—publishing nothing? Or like the German poet Rilke, described here in Kathleen Spivack's poem, "Straining"? Or Joyce, who came here to Paris to write about Dublin? Or Hemingway? Orwell? The beat writers? Or George Whitman, whose Shakespeare and Company bookshop is stuffed with the typed one-page autobiographies of aspiring writers who've stayed there?

One thing is certain—Paris is seen as *the* place to come and write. And that attracts writers. And when you attain a critical mass of writers you have a scene, a community of writers sharing their work, learning from each other, honing the craft. And the thing has the potential to snowball. In this anthology we've collected some voices from the latest generation of that scene and some older voices who all have a relationship with Paris. John Berger reflects on his initiation into books as a means to learn about how to live, under the guidance of his *passeur*, a former inhabitant of Paris. Some of our other writers have found in Paris a distance from home that allows them to look back and write about where they're from. In this vein we have Andrea Jonsson's "Yellow Rusted Truck" and Neil Uzzell's short fiction about growing up in the American South. Also Isabel Harding's story of awkwardness, suburban boredom, and breaking into swimming pools in "Zombie Mermaid."

Yet we also have stories set in Paris that describe aspects of what it is like to live here. Jeffrey Greene's "Cooking Octopus with Madame Esteves" does this with humour. Marty Hiatt has his own off-kilter view of Paris in his disoriented pieces. In "She always reads the last line first," I've tried to capture some of the romance of the city in a more real way than the postcards and the black-and-white photos everyone puts on their walls.

Other Paris stories here are Marie Davis and Margaret J. Hults's "A Castle for

Simone," notable for its spontaneity, its balance of modern fairytale darkness with joy and at least the possibility of love. Jonathan Hamrick's "Among Other Things" spins off from a Paris laundrette and a series of imagined "What ifs" into an encounter between two men described with rare depth. A very different voice belongs to Helen Cusack O'Keeffe, whose extract "The Ehrlich Remedy for Grief" has one eyebrow distinctly raised in its take on the nineteenth-century novel. I can't think of anyone else in Paris or elsewhere writing like her or taking so much obvious pleasure in it. And in this brief discussion of the prose in this book I haven't even yet mentioned the poetic-meditative writing of Alexander Maksik, or the writing on pain and dysfunctional relationships of Sion Dayson. Or Julie Kleinman and Jessica Malcomson's very different takes on twenty-first-century relationships— Julie Kleinman's downbeat and almost nostalgic, Jessica Malcomson's hedonistic, lost, searching.

All these writers have chosen to come live on the periphery of the English-language publishing world, at least for a while. Why? It's not only the legend of Paris as the place to try to write, as the place to escape to to live an exciting, meaningful life. (Recently seen in the film *Revolutionary Road*). Once you're in Paris, the physical and cultural distance from home can be an advantage—here you may gain an outside perspective from which to look back and see home more clearly. And the pressure is off, you're away from the competition back home. And where certainly in England attempts to write are seen as pretentious and/or foolish ("You should be making money."), in France there's far more support and interest. Here, "intellectual" is not an insult. And so, to paraphrase Henry James, Paris can be like a womb in which to grow as a writer.

Shakespeare and Company, named after the original bookshop that published James Joyce's *Ulysses* in Paris in the twenties, is still going strong, despite its founder being in his nineties (his daughter Sylvia does most of the running of the shop these days.) The bookshop still draws people who feel that calling to write. They stumble in with some vague idea that this is the place to realize that dream and be a real writer. And, just as for Rilke in Kathleen Spivack's poem, the props are not enough. Writing is about learning the craft and honing one's talent, about reading everything to see how other people do it and writing, writing, writing until the craft is so in your being that it comes almost without thinking.

So what is the scene in Paris like right now? Its hubs are the independent bookshops, especially the anarchic Shakespeare and Company, The Red Wheelbarrow, The Abbey Bookshop, Berkeley Books, and the Village Voice. All these regularly have readings. Shakespeare and Co. now puts on a literary festival every two years that attracts the likes of Paul Auster, Hanif Kureishi, and Jeanette Winterson. Shakespeare and Co. also has an author reading at seven p.m. every Monday.

There are several series of poetry readings. Ivy Writers Paris does bilingual readings in French and English, with translations, to expose audiences to the sounds of both languages. They focus on experimental writing, often North American but also from as far east as Japan. There's a convivial atmosphere and afterwards the opportunity to go to dinner with the poets, including Jen K. Dick who co-runs it and also compiles the English listing of literary events in Paris on her blog, fragment78.

If narrative poetry is more your thing, try the weekly open mike series I've been running since 2006: Spoken Word Paris. All kinds of poetry and short prose are welcome, and readers/performers sign up on the night and get five minutes to make the words come alive. It's not a competition, it's more performance poetry in the open spirit of a beatnik coffeehouse or an English pub poetry night.

WICE runs a long-standing series of poetry readings in conjunction with their excellent Paris-based magazine *Upstairs at Duroc*, which takes place mostly at Berkeley Books. Double Change is a series with a similar taste in poets to Ivy Writers, but it's more aimed at French speakers. Everything is translated. It was founded by two professors of English and American literature, Vincent Broqua and Olivier Brossard. They put out CDs and an online journal.

The longest running series was the Live Poets Society, put on for fourteen years by John Kliphan to give poetry a voice. It featured native English speakers but also many poets writing in English as a second language. This series has ended but is being revived in a new form by Dylan Harris as Poets Live. He's looking particularly for readings from poets who are visiting Paris.

Writers' workshops and groups have exploded since 2003 when I couldn't find a single one and so started my own weekly drop-in at Shakespeare and Company: the Other Writers' Group. Two big annual events have long been the Paris Poetry Workshop in May, run by poet Cecilia Woloch, and the Paris Writers' Workshop in July run by WICE. Both workshops feature some of the published writers who live in Paris. Alice Notley was this year's poet-in-residence at the Paris Writers' Workshop. WICE also runs writing classes throughout the year.

There are French festivals that bring in North American authors, which reflect a new focus on getting these voices translated into French. Corti Editions has put out translations of Cole Swensen and has a book of translation of Robert Duncan forthcoming.

And finally, as well as *Upstairs at Duroc*, which is published in Paris, there are also European journals in English with Parisian authors working on them; for example, *nthposition* (Rufo Quintavalle) and *versal* (Jen K. Dick).

All that is to say that there is a vibrant scene in Paris, with many ways into it.

POEMS & PROSE

RUFO QUINTAVALLE

Joined-up writing

Perhaps I've lived in Paris too long
but I'm getting to like
the unauthorized lawn,
the sense of edges, of each thing
having its place;

poems as rocks,
not soil.

As cities go

It's not a bad place, Paris, as cities go,
a ballast of tradition but that's Europe for you;

not a bad place to live, plenty of quiet to think in
if you avoid the scrum and pouting zoo of fashion,

but still I am lonely
for Burnside's suburbs, Murray's sprawl.

They say there are catacombs underneath the theatres,
but I know if I found them they'd vanish like in Fellini.

After Rimbaud

I is not enough;
if cock be crayon
you be the rainbow

29/09/08

The park bench hums

could be the metro
or a muscle cramp

then stops

& train & spasm
vanish

JORIE GRAHAM

Dawning

I do not kill the spider. I do not waste
                              the other side of the paper. Where the fires
                              are terrifying the penned-in
horses, I try to give my mind to the horses. Where there is no more water—and none
                              can be gotten anywhere
                              anymore—I try to send to that moment
                              in history
this water. I open the spigot, run it over my hands, cup them, feel it flow away
                              over these glowing
palms. And bend to it. And put my eyes and mouth
                              in my water in my
                              hands. In there
                              the soldier is still leaning up to me in astonishment
                              as we both see his
                              legs gone,
                              and are
for the briefest instant before the pain and the rest of life, are
                              there, there is no
sound, we are, with everything else that is in this fire, blinking, astonished,
                              we stare at each other,
                              at the whole planet
                              in the horse's eye,
at the spider whose web is jittery in rising smoke, at the blank paper—what is it we
                              would still
                              write down I think
in my part of the long held-breath stare in which no sound—no—correction
                              just before a moment ago

                    the bell in the nearby
                    church rang and for
                    the first time
I could hear as if the inside of the cast-iron thing,
                    and its being struck was
                    dull, and the smallness
                    of the sound
                    cast out by the
                    steeple
                    into its large surrounding fields
was thin, was full of the simplicity of cast iron and no more, was
                    iron's telling of iron's

tale—and you could hear the beading of seams in the interior curve, the tapping of
                    hammers upon it when
                    molten—
the being deep in earth the being torn out and smelted and cast and
                    welded and then re-
paired again, again, until no further transformation is possible—the earth has been entered, its
                    contents
                    removed, given
                    form,
                    extreme
                    heat—and it is delivered into
                    a belief
                    system—
                    which sounds the notes
                    in this order—the whole song of iron and
nothing else after the silence begins again and in it one

cock crowing in mist, another, a third,

their voices harsh,

low, full of attempted

rise—again, again,

the attempted rise of throat and chest—and the four low-cutting notes of daybreak—

and what now remains of him loosening its first moan, face to face, warning of something—

that the sun is arriving perhaps?—archaic, stone-

filled—

gathered round the final one unspooling peal—

and I watch the spider in dust, in wind—and I see

horizon begin

its tissued clarifying

again—

such that form

will soon

enter world

anew—and gather round us its rememberment—and yet, for now, just now, these creatures each

singing as if each

alone their

growl and crackle and break and fall and drift and stare and

brazenness, surenesses,

absolutely no impatience,

no rose of sound, no

quivering—

you could hear it as dark wasted blood—wasted as no one is

noticing—no one is

there to see the

throat being cut, so it just leaks and pools

and dries, and it is

                 that sound,

                 fate's sound,

                 a gut breaking out and

                 trying to make it rise—

                 always this desire to rise, to

bloom. Is there nothing that is content to be still. Is there nothing that will

                 stay in the bowels of earth,

                 unsaid, unfound, un-

changed—is there nothing that will *not waken*—but

                 look—it all breaks

                 out—it all wants to be in

the marketplace the war the wheel the flapping of flags the sounding of the clock the

                 wing-beating of

                 wind—where blades flash and we

call it daybreak—where the gaping of point of view opens—and look here they come

                 out of the caves

into the clearing—here they come carrying huge blocks of stone to make their shrine—

                 some are masters some are slaves—

the bell the spider the horse the crow-in-with-wind the iron the web the horizon

                 sending me its firming of out-

                 line, the first row of

                 trees advancing my way as

trees, the legs elsewhere than the body

                 which day shall illumine and point to

saying, there, too late, way too

                 late, then the beginning of

                 the next row of

trees, and some diagonals which shall in an instant be rooftops, and then the village, and

                    now by my
                    window, as if a crime I
have just this second pen-in-hand remembered I committed last night,
                    truth slices the burlap
                    sack of the end of night
open, and leaks its icy—ah—its hate and gorgeousness—oh no here is life I think unable
                    to step aside its bullet it
                    comes
into the human heart—there is no stopping it—infected with beauty—and the doorways
                    are filling, and the windows are opening, and the
                    desire for an idol leads
                    us again into the
                    burning web
which is day.

Jorie Graham

On the virtue of a dead tree

And that you hold the same one hawk each day I pass through my field
                                        up. And that it
                                        may choose its
                                        spot so
freely, from which to scan, and, without more than the wintry beguiling
                                        wingstrokes seeding
                                        the fields of air,
swoop. It feeds. There is no wasteland where the dead oak
                                        lives—my
                                        darling—up-
start vines on its trunk, swirling in ebblight, a desert of gone-silent
                                        cells—where another force is
                                        gleaming—tardy—
waning—summer or winter no longer
                                        truths, no prime, no
                                        year, no day where sun
                                        exists—
just a still-being-here in this small apparently silent multitudinous world of
                                        infinite yearning and
                                        killing and
sprouting—even now at the very start of the season—lengthening, in-
                                        visible in their
                                        cracking open of
pod—and push—like the first time we saw each other you and I—
                                        impatient immediately . . .
Blackness is the telephone wire—blackness the blissless instant-
                                        communication,

the twittering poverty killing behind and beneath and deep at the core of

each screen, end-

less, someone breaking someone's

fingers—just now—hear their laughter—everyone in their prison—there in their human

heart which

they cannot

for all the parting of flesh with

cement-sluiced rubber

hose—and even the axe to the heart—reach—the fantasy of independence—es-

cape. It wants them. It wants them to

fly inside it. "Fly" it screams

taser in

hand. Prison is never

going to be

over. Day as it breaks is the principal god, but with the hood on they cannot

know this. Till it is finally sliced open the

beating heart. Loved

ones shall pay

ransom

for the body of

their child. To this, friend, the hero is the dead tree. Here in my field, mine.

I have forced it. I have paid for it. My money like a wind flowing over it.

Have signed the paperwork and seen my name there. And a cloud

arrives from the East

into it. And the prison

grows too large to see.

And it does not sing, ever,

my silent hawk, always there when I arrive, before it startles, on its chosen

branch. And I think of

the dead-through trunk, the leafless limbs, the loosening of the
                                 deep-drying roots in the
living soil. And I slow myself to extend love to them. To their as-
                                 yet-still-sturdy
                                 rotting, and how they hold
                                 up this grey-blue
                                 poverty of once-sapflowing
                                 limbs, their once everywhere-turning branchings,
for my small hungry creature to glide from in his silence
                                 over the never-for-an-instant-not-working
                                 rows of new
                                 wheat. It is
good says my human soul to the crop. I will not listen for
                                 song anymore. I will
listen for how dark comes-on to loosen the cringing wavering
                                 mice from their dens and
how they creep up to the surfaces and out onto the surfaces and
                                 how the surfaces
yield their small grey velvet barely visible in the last glow
                                 to that part of the world
the dead tree sends forth. I have lived I
                                 say to the evening.
I have plenty of anger and am good and dry with late-breaking news. I
                                 am living.
And the iron door of the night creeps and clicks. And the
                                 madness of the day
hangs around restless at the edges of the last visible leaves
                                 with a reddish glow
                                 and moves them with tiny

                              erratic swiftnesses and
the holy place shuts, baggy with evening, and here it is
                              finally night
                              bursting open
with hunt.

Sundown

Sometimes the day
                    light winces
                    behind you and it is
a great treasure in this case today a man on
                    a horse in calm full
                    gallop on Omaha over my
                    left shoulder coming on
                    fast but
calm not audible to me at all until I turned back my
                    head for no
                    reason as if what lies behind
                    one had whispered
"what can I do for you today" and I had just
                    turned to
                    answer and the answer to my
answer flooded from the front with the late sun he/they
                    were driving into—gleaming—
                    wet chest and upraised knees and
light-struck hooves and thrust-out even breathing of the great
                    beast—from just behind me,
                    passing me—the rider looking straight
                    ahead and yet
smiling without looking at me as I smiled as we
                    both smiled for the young
                    animal, my feet in the
breaking wave-edge, his hooves returning, as they begin to pass
                    by,

to the edge of the furling
break, each tossed-up flake of
ocean offered into the reddish
luminosity—sparks—as they made their way,
boring through to clear out
life, a place where no one
again is suddenly
killed—regardless of the "cause"—no one—just this
galloping forward with
force through the low waves, seagulls
scattering all round, their
screeching and mewing rising like more bits of red foam, the
horse's hooves now suddenly
louder as it goes
by and its prints on
wet sand deep and immediately filled by thousands of
sandfleas thrilled to the
declivities in succession in the newly
released beach—just
at the right
moment for some
microscopic life to rise up through these
cups in the hard upslant
retreating ocean is
revealing, sandfleas finding them just as light does,
carving them out with
shadow, and glow on each
ridge, and
water oozing up through the innermost cut of the

hoofsteps,
and when I shut my eyes now I am not like a blind person
walking towards the lowering sun,
the water loud at my right,
but like a seeing person
with her eyes shut
putting her feet down
one at a time
on the earth.

Straining

Sojourning alone in Paris,
he thought, now finally
he was a poet. All the props
were his: the cloak, the hat
like a cringing accordion,
the moustache, the walking stick
pronouncing ends-of-sentences
on the sidewalk.

Only he had not reckoned
on the loneliness. Isolate,
terrible as a lavatory,
it chilled him, coming in from
the warm purple streets.
His room lay in the darkness
like a terrapin, promising nothing.

Something unseen, a posterity,
crouched in the corners, watching,
ticking off his movements: his forearms
as he washed his shirt
in the basin; the casual
lighting of a match. That eerie tiger
noticed everything. His neck
prickled at his writing stand.

If you love me, guard
my solitude, he wrote
to endless mistresses, his wife,
his friends. Solitude!
It is the sallow wallpaper
of furnished rooms.
Worried as a snail, he worked,
extruding a thin slimy track.

While to him a young man
earnestly wrote: *Dear Mr. Rilke,*
how shall I become a poet,
having a most desperate longing
to do so, and in my bosom
some small songs?

And like a garden, the replies
profused, lavishing
in leaking roses, borders
of bachelor's-buttons, blue
at the buttonhole,
and the scent of solitary
sentry lilies: sentences
burgeoning like blood from a slit
artery.

No tourniquet could stanch it.
The heart, spurting, sprinted
onto the page. *Dear Mr. Kappus . . .*

Loneliness, that leech obscene
on his mouth, was sucking,
glutting out whole sonnets,
clots of sound.

Monet's Path

You walk into the painting,
you walk down the path
through the bleached grass toward the village:
the cicadas are singing;
you are going someplace

ordinary.
Perhaps it is to the post office,
perhaps it is to get milk;
the dry grasses are hardly stirring:
a museum guard is at standstill, watching you.

You walk next to poplar trees,
you walk through sun and shade:
it is an ordinary errand
but the flowers shriek, brighter than daytime,
and the weeds murmur: "notice me."

The painter is so much a part of this
the crickets hardly bother to silence themselves.
Nothing stops singing:
grass celebrates its green-ness
and the moist ground, underfoot.

springs back, debonair, as
you part it with your eye—it is almost
a feeling—this green dapple of light and shade,
framed, dazzling, just when you entered it.

Pale Light in the Luxembourg Garden

A pale watery light invades the trees
as if one were already reading
the *Book of One's Life.*—Afterwards.—
Was it like that? Was it really like that?
I remember holding you in my arms
but the etched intake of breath
has already faded, like a sepia photograph
in which posed strangers, frontal and solemn,
look out and beyond one, preternaturally still.

This season your lover is both
coming toward and receding. Tentative,
the bluish sky's an aquatint, a puff of breath
between stark sudden-springing branches.
All kinds of promises are not yet made,
diaphanous: hold on, hold back
before raw summer sears us in its blast

and irons down our (photocopied) past,
helplessly pressed
like leaves that blazed once, faraway,
emblemed in wax—(we had our day)—
between the pages of some dusty book
in which not even we, so faded now,
would ever care to look.

DAVID BARNES

She always reads the last line first

In the November morning, Notre Dame looks as if it has been cast from metal, not cut from pale stone. The slanting daylight picks out every detail, each carved saint and gargoyle. The taxi sprays rain from the asphalt covering the cobbles on the quai de la Tournelle. It's early. The Paris streets are empty. The white walls of the boulevards are wintry calm.

A girl in a red coat with black hair is standing waiting to cross the road. For a second I think it's Anna.

We draw level.

I'm wrong.

Something in me is always looking for her. For two years there's been a constant awareness of separation at the back of my mind. Of how close or how distant she is from me. It has a physicality that is so familiar that I can describe it precisely. It's like the tug of a thread fixed inside the back of my skull. Or, sometimes, like a sideways gravity pulling at my stomach, trying to haul me back into place, back to where I should be, to wherever she is.

Its effect is that whatever I'm doing, I'm distracted. Split between the here-and-now and the tension in my body created by her absence.

When I first stepped off the train in the lofty hall of the Gare du Nord, I thought I'd soon get itchy feet. But I got a job teaching English in a two-room school and I stayed. I was thirty-two. I taught English all year and on the last day of her course Anna suggested we all go for a drink.

The Lighthouse Café, Les Phares, sprawls outwards from under the iron-barred fortress of the Banque de France, on the site where the old Bastille stood—before the crowd demolished it so thoroughly that not a stone was left in place.

The tables are the tiny round ones all Parisian cafés have, just big enough for two people. Paris is a city geared to the I-you relationship, to assignations between two people, whether your encounter is with your friend, your father, or your lover. It lends itself to the revealing of confidences and to intimate storytelling.

Anna was then twenty-seven. She had a darting, bright energy overlaying sadness, as though she was temporarily escaping something. When she leaned forward to make a comment, or raised her wine glass to her lips, she moved with casual poise.

Her hair, straightened and dyed jet black, was twisted behind her head at the back and pinned with a Japanese hairstick. Her fringe fell across the sides of her pale face to the level of the mouth. Her teeth thrust forward slightly, parting her lips a little, as though she was about to taste or bite or kiss.

Her eyes were slightly too large for her thin face. She was too thin. Like my best friend when I was a boy, who was so thin that he turned blue in winter. The bone structure of her face and hands was visible in the same way his had been.

There were times I felt like her face was a mask. When she did something ordinary, making some small gesture or comment in the clichéd language of everyday speech, it came as a relief.

The other students left one by one. She stayed, as I hoped she would. She didn't sip her wine in a restrained way, was not careful to prevent it touching her lips. So it stained the corners of her mouth, her teeth. She spoke English, only switching to French when she couldn't find the words. Her Italian accent was so soft the waiter thought she was French.

It was just us.

We talked about books that had set us on fire. She was reluctant to leave, to go back to her flat, to the boyfriend she still lived with.

"*Je suis lourde*," she sighed. I am heavy. Her sadness was like a tangible weight. I knew she was not someone I should get involved with.

"Do you think being in love can ever last?" she asked.

"I think it always burns out."

"But it's our fault," she said earnestly. "When you first meet someone you really see them. But then you decide you know who they are and you stop looking. You stop seeing them anymore." She held her empty glass in a casual, offhand way. "If only you could see them with the same interest you had at the start, maybe it could last . . ."

The late evening traffic turned round the Column of the Place de la Bastille. The Column was the spoke of a wheel, the cars rumbled over the cobbles, a wheel turning in a staggered series of stop-starts.

"I don't want to go home yet," Anna said. "Let's go for a walk."

We wandered along the Boulevard Henri IV, crossed the bridge to the Île Saint-Louis. There were lights on the far side of the river. A series of amphitheatres have been cut out of the quay and in the summer musicians come there to play and people dance tango in the night air. As we crossed to the left bank, snatches of music came across the Seine and I saw the crowd whirling around on the edge of the black water.

Reaching the quay, Anna sat down on a grassy slope and looked out across the river. Her eyes shone.

"You can feel its breath," she said.

People were chatting on the stone steps of the amphitheatres or dancing. It was easy to talk, watching the black river flow. A fire juggler was practising in the dark. The grass felt rough under my hand.

We lay back on the grass in the cool July evening. I propped myself on one elbow, turned towards her. So close. I needed nothing more than to just let things unfold and flow. I didn't want this to end in just a kiss.

That August, Parisians abandoned their city to the tourists and fled on holiday. The avenues became hot, sweaty. The buildings so dazzlingly white that the glare hurt your eyes. Bakeries and bars closed for the entire month, the streets emptied. Paris breathed.

Anna left for Portugal. I wandered down through Spain to Seville. Another white city, flatter than Paris, scorched by the sun, the ground sandy yellow. The broad sweep of the river evoking the coast. As though the city had been washed up on the beach and abandoned as driftwood, emptied of residents—they had migrated to the sea to escape the heat. I hung around, took a bus to Lisbon.

I met Anna, but she was with her boyfriend in the dying throes of their relationship. We drank in a bar high in the Bairro Alto, enjoying the cool night air after the heat of the day. I remember the three of us sitting with our backs against a wall in a narrow street busy with people. He was silent. She only talked to me. Around midnight it began to rain gently, just a soft mist. I touched her hand, the briefest caress.

Back in Paris she left me a message.

"Don't you feel something was missed?"

We met beside the Canal Saint-Martin and talked all afternoon in cafés, soaking up the last of the summer sun. Paris was full of people greeting old friends after a month or more apart. The day stretched out into evening dark.

We got the metro. She stood, holding onto the pole, swaying slightly with the movement of the train. I was afraid. If I kissed her, she might not kiss me back and it would all be over. Everything was like a dance around the possibility of that kiss.

So I said goodnight.

The next morning, I emerged from the metro at rue des Pyrénées, into brilliant sunshine. The steep street receded away to the left. I met Anna at the Parc des Buttes Chaumont and we climbed a path that wound up the hill. Through the trees I could see Paris laid out below us, stretching away to the Eiffel Tower.

We sat on the shaded grass, she looked at me.

I said, "I want to know what happens if I kiss you."

"So kiss me."

The pause before I kissed her is a still point in time that connects all that came before with all that followed.

Was it still possible to make a choice then? Or was the kiss and the two years that flowed from it inevitable?

Later she said, "If I kiss you, it's because I want to make love."

There was an urgency, yet paradoxically an effortlessness. When she touched her hand to my chest, I involuntarily held my breath, everything focussed down to that one sensation.

That night we went back to my flat. Her black hair the head of a burning match. It was as though something had broken open inside. I was thirsty for her tears, her sweat, the pulse of her blood, her joy.

I didn't ask about the boyfriend, I only cared that she was there. She went to lean out of the narrow balcony, the gauzy curtain blowing in the wind, the night flooding in around the paleness of her skin.

"So what happens now?" I asked.

She turned.

She saw me once more before leaving for her parents' to escape the flat she still shared with her ex. We made love in the afternoon. I discovered tiny birthmarks were scattered across her skin like brown pebbles. She left me at the steps to the metro and suddenly it began to rain, torrentially. Everyone in the street had to take shelter under the awnings and in the shops. The cafés filled up with dripping people talking loudly and cheerfully in this forced break. Soaking wet people dashed past outside the windows holding newspapers above their heads. The warmth came through the thick china of the espresso cup I held in my hand.

"What about your boyfriend?"

She sighed, didn't want to be reminded.

"It's over. I can't even kiss him."

"So tell him you're seeing someone."

"It's too soon. And we're still living together in the same tiny flat."

"Move out."

"It's not so easy, you know. You don't just snap your fingers and you find a flat in Paris."

We met for snatched hours a few times a week. She was always nervous that her ex would find out. And he was suspicious of her, asking questions. They fought.

I trusted her so I wasn't resentful. More bemused and lifted out of the ordinary by what was happening.

"I can't call you. I hardly see you," I told her. "It's like I have this girl who I'm really into, and yet at the same time I don't really have her."

She looked weary.

"Can you wait for me?"

"Don't make me wait too long."

"Just till I have my own place. Then we can really start."

I had this image of a bucket of water, full to the brim now, but the water was slowly running out through a hole in the bottom. When it had all run out, it would be too late. But most of the time then, I was still so high just to have found her.

"It's you I want," she told me. "I think about you all the time. I need to see you . . . But what am I doing, here, in Paris? Maybe I should leave, to Italy or Argentina . . ."

She looked at me, her glass of red wine in her hand. "Come with me?"

"To Argentina?"

I would have gone, just like that.

She didn't leave Paris. In the cold of November she found a flat in the twentieth *arrondissement*. The night I flew back from a friend's wedding, she was waiting for me there for the first time. She buzzed me into the staircase. It was seven floors up from the ground floor and I was hot and light-headed when I got to the top.

She stood there in the open doorway, smiling.

Both of us were nervous around each other. But I was sure.

Later, I said:

"You know that thing I didn't tell you, before I left, that I told you I'd tell you when I came back . . ."

"Yes?"

I said the words.

She grinned her wide smile.

Said the words.

A week later she phoned. Her tone was different

"I have to see you. Can you meet me?"

At six-thirty I closed the glass door of the Café de l'Industrie on the chilling air. The long bar was almost empty. Framed posters of old film stars lined the walls, a timeless clock with Chinese numerals and no hands was above the bar. She was sitting at the window, reading. She put her book down and kissed me. She looked anxious.

The waitress arrived just then, and Anna waited until she'd gone.

She took my hand, held it as though she needed to touch, as though it was precious.

"I thought I was ready."

There was no joy in her voice.

She looked up from my hand.

"I don't know if I want you, or I want to try again . . . with . . ."

I must've looked sad. I looked away, out of the window at someone cycling up the street, their fluorescent jacket.

"If I had to choose now, I'd choose you. But I don't know if I'd choose you in the future."

I had the unreal sensation of trying to walk through quicksand.

"I really thought everything would be okay once I had my own place and I could just see you, but it's not."

She sighed. The wine glasses stood uselessly on the table. Someone else came into the bar behind me.

"Are you seeing him?" The words were strangely easy to say, but foreign, as if someone else was saying them.

"I saw him on Tuesday."

"Did you kiss him?"

She paused before shaking her head.

Light spilled onto the dark grain of the wooden table from the dimmed lamps along the bar. Night had arrived outside, with that suddenness of November. How cozy it could have been.

"It's just too soon," she said painfully.

"You can't choose when you meet someone."

She looked down at her glass, then back at me. Touched my hand again. Her fingers were always cold.

So I told her my stories. I made up stories about her. In the dimly lit crowded bars, in the evenings.

"I can see you in a film, early colour, a sixties historical epic set in Spain. You'd be the tragic heroine, who suffers anguish, who dies at the very end."

The words came so easily. All the things I'd longed to say to someone, I said to her. Words sustained us.

The only time she could really give herself to me was when we made love. "*Je suis ta chose*," she whispered late at night in her cold flat. She was almost invisible, lit only by the streetlight through the slats in the blind, only by the moon.

Sometimes I'd wake and she'd be gone, smoking in the darkness of the other room. "I hate your sleep," she said. "You don't stay with me."

Je suis ta chose. I'm your thing.

Hasty minutes in the café bright with morning before riding the metro to work, tired but elated. Every caress told me she was in love with me. I would coast for days.

And then she'd be gone again.

"It's not fair on you," she'd say. "I can't give you what you want. I wish I could, really."

In April, we stopped.

That lasted three weeks, before she left a message.

"Would it be so wrong just to see you?"

But of course we didn't just see each other, we picked up right where we'd left off. Three weeks of separation had only built up the charge to a higher voltage. We discharged that tension through our bodies.

But nothing had changed. So we stopped again. For three weeks. And again.

A year after that first drink, we met again at Les Phares.

"I'm not someone you should see," she said. "*Je suis un piège pour toi.*" I am a trap for you.

The cars spun round the Place de la Bastille, the rush hour traffic roaring. The Place slopes up to the column in the centre, making you feel that you're slightly sunk down. We sat side by side, facing the monument and not each other.

"I can't do this," she said.

That familiar feeling of sinking, on the edge of shock.

"You'll start to hate me."

"Not yet."

That bucket of water with the hole, the water running out.

"Stay."

"I can't," she said guiltily. "I have work tomorrow. I'd have to get up at six . . ."

But she came back to mine. I eased her out of her loose jeans, laid her down on the bed.

After making love she lay beside me, facing away. I traced my finger down the lizard vertebrae of her spine. It was past midnight, the last metro left in twenty minutes.

"If I was your girlfriend you would get bored of me." She sighed, stretched her arms casually upward. "I can't see it ever lasting."

I sat up. Everything had stopped. Back leant against the wall, I stared straight ahead.

"Breathe," she said, alarmed. "You're not breathing."

I didn't see her again till the end of the summer. Went to her friend's party. She leaned back against the open kitchen window, drunk, wearing ridiculous pink furry boots. Holding on to me.

"I think . . ." she said, echoing the song on the stereo, "I think I'm ready . . ." She swung herself forward. "Trust me," she said. "It can't be over because I can't stop thinking about you. Trust me."

Spring. The sky swept the trees above the tables outside the Lieu Dit restaurant. It was cold. My T-shirt was too thin. The few scattered days of warmth had not transformed into the long delayed summer. I looked at Anna and the trees bursting with new leaves, their branches whipped in the wind overhead. New growth stems, with huge leaves like veined sails, were being broken off and littered the gutters along the boulevard, got tangled against the legs of the chairs.

"It feels like being on a train that's going faster and faster and heading for a crash," I said. "It isn't going to stop. The only thing to do is to jump from the moving train."

She twisted her scarf with her fingers.

"I'm fighting against you," she said. "Against being with you."

"Why? Why fight it?"

"Because I *can't* be with you. I just can't."

She fumbled for a cigarette.

It was hard to say the words that needed to be said.

So she said them.

"We have to stop."

I do not want to write poetry or eat at the Bistro du Peintre.

So many things to put away, to hide. I used to look for signs. Tried to interpret what she said and did, a running search through a labyrinth of second guesses. Among the six billion people in the world, there are so few that I can respond to as I can her. I cannot choose them. Those few, they are so vast that they are all I can contain.

I remember lying awake watching her, her lips parted slightly in sleep. So many details to forget. She always carries a book with her. She always reads the last line first.

this bird

this bird, this black scrap nailed to the air

only this bird, like fluff caught on barbed wire

that is not there

feathers like burnt leaves, he hangs

battling the wind that textures the air

flickering black paper pegged to nothing

he folds himself into a stone and falls

LISA PASOLD

Ocular

you get off the airplane and the following morning you see huge black spots floating in your eyesight. this is a bad sign, you think, or is this simply the jetlag people complain about? maybe your eye has been pierced by beauty too literally.

while you are eating your croissant, awkwardly as you can't see it properly though the taste is flakey as it should be, you remember your sister and her eye surgery five years ago, you thought it was cataracts and she said no not at all. so you phone her, long-distance, forgetting the time change and you wake her up and she says, well, sounds like your retina has torn.

then you are in the emergency room of the hospital, trying to understand what the doctor is telling you. "*Bienvenue en France!*" he says cheerfully, "we will take the middle route for surgery. it is *urgent.*" this sounds more like the word "unguent," which is less worrying to you than the word "urgent" might be.

but after the surgery, there are four specks in your eye. puzzling, along with the large grey mass which is hopefully supposed to fade. "*Mais oui,*" the doctor says, when you ask about the four specks, "those are the stitches. We sewed the retina on again for you, it seemed a good idea."

ah, you nod, wondering if you've misunderstood the language. "You cannot be flying or scuba diving," the doctor says, touching your eyelashes. the scuba wasn't on your Paris must-see tourism list, but the flying? you explain that you live in D.C. and the flight home's next Thursday.

"No, no flying, three weeks." or does he say three months? you are distracted by his beauty. you can't be sure what he's said, after you walk out of the examining room,

58

Lisa Pasold

and the prospect of walking back up those hospital front stairs with the handrail, not being able to see properly, no, it's all too much.

so from your hotel room, you phone your real doctor back in the States and ask her. she tells you it's entirely your choice, up to you, three weeks should be okay. "A-O-K," she laughs, "probably a reasonable risk."

this is my eye, you say, what do you mean by reasonable?

so you are at a picnic now, by the Seine, which flows to the Atlantic and if you were a salmon, you could swim home, maybe. aren't there salmon back in the Seine, wasn't that the headline, the day your retina decided to detach? you can't remember the newspaper article, you were a bit distracted that morning, what with the jetlag and the beauty and all. but you're wondering whether three weeks will be adequate, or will you need to stay for three months, which seems a long time? but maybe not so bad. it would be nice to see the Seine in different kinds of weather.

and if it's three months, will you fall in love with the doctor, try to explain American politics to him? lean into another glass of wine and laugh about the dining room table you have yet to assemble, think of the long heavy box, all that wood veneer leaning flat against the wall of your brand-new condominium in Washington, D.C., because it takes two people to put together a dining room, you tell the doctor, especially if you only have one eye.

"But you have two lovely eyes," the doctor says, and you find yourself telling your friends you are stuck in Paris, you cannot leave, only to hear them say Sure, you're Stuck in Paris, Sure You Are.

you say, no, really, I can't fly, I'm not allowed to fly. even though every day, it seems to you, something else goes flying away from you, a floater careening past your flawed but trusting eyes.

Getting the bends at the Hotel du Petit Canard

this fugue.
your feet on the piano pedal in those too small shoes.
the green of your dress delights me with what might be insects thrilling
with concert cacophony—because it glitters, that sound,
because it is a rope
because it is your throat.

I'll be in the fur hat at the stage door at midnight.
you say a musician's life
is like diving, a girl can get the bends
from these changes in depth. while you check in
to the Hotel Georges V,
your green sequined dress with the view—someone's
Eiffel Tower. the Bösendorfer piano tuned,
polished. applause evaporates
so quickly. two days later the gig is done. everything
that came easily, you give away in handfuls,

until you're back in the room I rent by the month
on the backside
of Sacré Coeur. real fucking cheap, you shrug, but no piano,
playing chords on the edge of the cigarette-scarred bedside table.

sometimes it is not enough to be tired; the world still has plans for you.
those kicked-off green shoes are so ill-suited to walking,
unlike a foot from any species. I am lying
on this empty rug while you practise

silent chords. it's more like tremors.
it's more like ice cream.

because you can't afford your own piano, even the practice rooms
are overpriced. you'd have to take the metro halfway across town
through all that silence.
you cannot change what's underneath,
melting. I better enjoy this arpeggio slide
because it's all I get from you
and then you're gone.

SUZANNE ALLEN

An Hour with Madame Sabatier[2]

True art, when it happens to us,
challenges the "I" that we are.

—Jeanette Winterson, *Art Objects*

Mistress to many, including her sculptor,
and muse   to Baudelaire,
she lies
stretched across a bed   of flowers carved
as intricately as her sinewy locks, her
parted lips—in French she whispers
décadence, punition.

Objectification circa eighteen forty-seven—
torso twisted, head thrown
back in that way that intensifies
climax, marketability, by simply elongating
the neck.   Cliché that I
am drawn to her. Temptation—
serpent bangled round one wrist,
her gown   falling softly away—
marble complexion   cold,   waist
kinked in a fine crease—flawless—breasts full;
otherwise   sexless.

---

2   *Femme piquée par un serpent*, Auguste Clésinger, Musée D'Orsay.

A husband listens to his audio guide.
      Obscene
critiques his wife as he lingers.

A mother explains to a four-year-old girl:
She didn't want to live—
Why?   The girl asks why.
She was so sad   having been separated
from her lover.   How death can look like
pleasure on a woman—
but she doesn't get into that.

Seine Scene

Two bicycles lie
At the curb on the quay where
A couple stands in the dirt, which grows
A tall now leafless tree
Silently (because
The window is closed and they
Are across the wide street. The bicycles,
The tree, two lovers, and the Seine
Behind them, green.)

They embrace, release, embrace again
And again, his face changing
Places from over her left
Shoulder, her right, over
And over again.
Until it becomes clear—
Not his face but the fact that she's not
Embracing him back. Arms at her side
Then flapping, her hand to her head,
Then gestures to the south and west
Across the water.

He looks and shrugs, gestures back,
Hugs her again. She flaps some more
Like a wounded bird fallen
From the tall tree, shoulders slumped
At the same time. He takes a step

Back and looks at her face.
She looks at the ground.
Not a sound from here. *"Cheri,"*
I imagine he says, but maybe
It's "Babe," or "Honey" instead.

Her nose and cheeks are
February red, though it is only November.
Her eyes visibly wet though the rain
Has let up. His lips
Do not smile. She goes
For her Velib, holding the handlebars
Firm, she resists some more as he
Tries again then gives in, lifting
His blue bike ready
To take the lead again.

Outside In

The café has a happy-hour
crowd. They smoke and offer up
their pocket change, drink standing at the bar.
Inverted in the silver glass on ceilings
and supports are people as they pass
so that I see them twice, three times, or four,
or just their heads—their hurried steps
muffled in February snow
to shuffles only heard when someone comes
or leaves. The swinging door is glass, both push
and pull the way the foreign language
does at lips and cheeks and
eyes around the room. The windows
frame Les Invalides—its great,
gold dome.

Hospitable, the demitasses, saucers
sing the barman's song. He stacks them high
and whistles so as not to have to speak
and fills my glass at just a nod—but
as I do, I catch the top of someone's head
deep in the mirrors—a dark-haired, balding man
is standing somewhere near. I see him there,
then here, and think it's you until
I find his face.

I never guessed
your thinning hair would be the thing
I missed and thought
I saw amidst a foreign crowd
that turned my insides
out.

ANDREA JONSSON

Yellow Rusted Truck

We started out around four p.m. after cold KFC and took our diet Pepsi refills in the yellow rusted truck. I put the car seat in the back and rigged an old T-shirt at the window for shade. The baby was sleeping, his neck bent rubbery, head lying against his left shoulder. With no AC I hoped it wasn't going to be a long trip. Mom bought gas, cigarettes, and white powdered doughnuts at the Sinclair on the way out of town. By then it was 97 degrees, the heat punching down, mirages rising off everything.

"Mom, don't you think it's too hot to go now? What if the car overheats?"

"You know I can't drive at night. Now get in."

As we pulled onto the freeway, the windows were open on both sides and the hair that escaped my ponytail whipped around my face stinging my eyes, tearing violently, loud and out of control. We didn't talk or put on the radio because we wouldn't have been able to hear. The open windows created a loud rhythmic suction and I kept having to open my mouth wide to un-pop my ears from the pressure.

It had been a while since we went on a road trip together. We had gone camping about every weekend in the summers until the baby was born. We even went during the school year, picking a different adventure, loading the tent and coolers in the back and hitting the road before the sun went up on Saturday mornings. But this was different. Mom hadn't told me where we were going. I felt like a little kid again, letting her take care of things. I relaxed into the loud heat. The baby was asleep and I wasn't going to need to navigate. I looked out the window thinking of nothing, the highway stretched out in front of us and was lost between the folds of mountains swallowing the pass. I turned around again to look at my son. My son. *I'm a mother*, I thought. It felt strange, but good. Even the heads that shook with disappointment at the grocery store didn't bring me down. They didn't know that my baby didn't need anything. He had two mothers.

Completely relaxed into his car seat he looked all snuggled in like a pit does when you first cut a peach in half. I took the leftover slivers of ice out of the Pepsi cups, rubbed them as they melted through my fingers then put my cold hands on Little Bear's forehead. Mom punched in the cigarette lighter under the Pepsi cup.

"Do you have to smoke with Little Bear in the car?" I asked her. She looked at me but I couldn't see her eyes through her dark sunglasses. She smirked.

"You think I don't know you smoke?" she said with her cigarette clamped between her teeth. I shook my head and turned to look at the baby. She had the cigarette pack stretched toward me. I slid one out.

"Feels like God's already blowing his smoke into the car, it's so goddamn hot."

The lighter clicked hot. Mom didn't reach for it immediately, she took the unlit cigarette out of her mouth and it caught a little where her lip had been wet.

"I'm not going to judge you," she said, her voice fighting against the wind. I took the lighter and lit my cigarette, then hers. The red glow against my face made my skin feel tight. I held the lit cigarette by the ashtray, but couldn't take a drag. The wind sucking through the cab smoked it. Mom held her cigarette in her mouth as she was driving through the pass. Little flakes of ash caught in her hair and melted into the sweat on her chest and she didn't wipe them away. She kept both hands on the steering wheel.

"It wasn't hot like this when you were a baby," she said.

The pass was dangerous. Little white crosses littered both sides of the road at the end of black brake marks. It was like some clumsy hand had taken thick black crayons to draw random parallel lines leading off the road. When Mom had finished smoking, she tossed her butt out the window. That made me mad, because the grass was so yellow and it would be just like her to cause some brush fire just because she didn't think to put it out first. Mine was crushed safely in the ashtray.

"There weren't as many forest fires when I was a baby either," I said.

She smiled. "Think of it as me burning up the past."

I watched the wind in the grass on the hills. Every now and then I held my head out of the window to blow my hair back. It wasn't often we drove out on the pass. I didn't even know the truck could go this fast anymore. We passed the Frontage Road exit, then slowly came through the mountains on the other side. Outside of Livingston, with the mountains not protecting us anymore, the wind suddenly came swatting at us across the highway. Mom had trouble controlling the truck.

"Wooo!" She laughed nervously. I braced myself and looked at the baby. He had moved a bit but was still asleep. I rearranged his collar kind of wishing he'd wake up. I wondered what he was dreaming of then, what stayed in his little memory that came back as dreams. Sometimes I would sit and watch him for hours as he slept, reading all of the expressions that came back over his face as though he was reliving the day. His face could change from laughing to terrified in a matter of seconds.

There were old bloodstains splattered all over the highway. Growing up it was a game we'd play—who could correctly identify the roadkill. But mom had never liked to play.

"You guys are sick," she would say. But she always knew what animal it was

As we drove, I saw three deer, bloated with their tongues out. I even saw a red fox with a bushy tail—the kind from cartoons. My eyes caught on a billboard shouting "COME SEE OUR REAL LIVE GRIZZLIES!" And then a couple of minutes later we drove past the valley with an actual makeshift Grizzly zoo. Behind chainlink fences were clods of cement in hilly shapes with square holes that were supposed to be caves' openings. I could see the bears over top of the barriers.

"God, how cruel," I said as we passed them.

"Not really," Mom answered even though I wasn't really talking to her. "They would probably be shot anyway. Those bears are already addicted to garbage and people. Those Grizzlies looking for easy food—they're the most dangerous." She looked into the rearview mirror at the baby and then at me. "So they give them to places like those instead of shooting them or moving them to Alaska." I didn't know if she was just trying to get under my skin, baiting me, or if she really thought that.

"I'd rather be shot," I said and she laughed and tapped my thigh.

"I doubt that," she said. "At least it's a life."

The sun went from hot on my arm to blinding, a huge orange orb in the rearview mirror. The reflection was so bright that Mom asked me to put my hand over it so she could see the road. We were driving due east and out of the mountains the highway stretched out and was lost on the horizon. Ahead pink hills cut into mines were crawling with trucks carrying dust and sand the colour of nail polish. Oil pumps pulled from the earth like sex and pendulums. The hills changed from yellow to green to blue in the shadows, to pink. Long car shadows overtook us and rumbled past. The cigarette lighter clicked and the sun burned into the backs of our heads.

When we turned off the freeway, Mom rolled up her window and motioned for me to do the same. There was a sudden vacuum silence in the cab.

"What do you remember about Dad?" she asked suddenly after continuing onto a road I didn't know. Her voice was thick and far away. I was surprised and a little uncomfortable. In twelve years she had mentioned him just twice, the first time two days before. And how like her, to pop out with a question that has no answer with hills whipping past and more roadkill than people.

"Uh, not much, I mean he left when I was six, Mom," I answered, hoping she wouldn't press.

"Oh, come on, you must remember something. You probably remember how his feet smelled? So bad!" She laughed and continued to look at me through her black sunglasses in the rearview mirror. The sun hit them from the side and I could see the outline of her eyes under the glare. It was weird, her trying to make it funny.

"Okay," I sighed. "His feet no, but he smelled like—something sweet. Like warm grass . . . and peanuts." I paused hoping that would be enough.

"Do you remember what he looked like?" she asked. For years my missing dad had been the enemy. Now I was forced to reminisce.

"I remember his braids and his rough face," I said, wondering where this was going. I thought she had wanted me to forget.

"He tied his braids together at the end and it reminded me of jump ropes. He was really big. That's about all." I rolled down the window. The cab of the car was taken over by the wind again for a while. I thought maybe she had gotten Dad out of her system.

"He really loved you girls." She sounded sad. I didn't want to talk about it anymore. But she continued.

"I remember everything about him, the shape of his fingernails, the colour of his eyelashes as they bleached toward the tips. I still see his naked pockmarked shoulders and the spaces in his teeth." She sighed. "It was so long ago but I remember everything." Was this mom? This poetic, nostalgic person next to me? I didn't want to know more. I was afraid she would talk about my sister who suddenly, by not being mentioned, took up all the breathable air.

I turned around and saw my baby's brown eyes open and silent. He never really cried.

"Hey Little Bear!" I said and smiled, glad to have an excuse not to talk about Dad anymore. He reached his hands out, wanting to be picked up. I undid my seatbelt and turned around to get him.

"He had to be on the reservation," Mom said, ignoring my baby talk as I lifted Little Bear onto my lap and gave him a dusted off doughnut.

"What?" I asked.

"He needed to feel the support of his tribe. It was hard for him in town. Most everyone thought he should try to blend in. You remember. He couldn't even cut his hair. He loved you girls so much it hurt, but after what happened to your sister he just couldn't take it. People talk about depression a lot. And you see those ads on TV. But what they don't say is that it's an incredibly painful illness. And it can't just be cured with drugs. It's real, and it's important that you understand that. He didn't leave because he didn't love you." Her voice was breaking. But she wasn't crying, just staring straight out the windshield with determination.

"Not everyone is as strong as you," I said, almost under my breath. She pretended not to hear me.

"I don't blame him anymore," she whispered.

What I remember of my sister I would never be able to tell her. She had become an idea, the sadness in my mother, the souvenir of everything bad. We had pictures so I would never forget what she looked like, hair curly but still thin like baby hair, eyes the colour of mom's. Through the pictures I remembered things like hugging her too hard. I remember being jealous. I remember that once, when she was sick, probably just with an ear infection or something, that it was serious enough to go to the hospital. Mom left me with the babysitter and I was so worried that I couldn't stop crying. Maybe I knew what was coming.

I bounced the Little Bear on my lap. We passed Horse Ranch Road exit, another swollen deer. Mom squinted. My sister sang through the hubcaps.

"I remember everything from then . . ." She paused as though wanting to say more. I let her take her time.

"But . . . I don't remember last weekend," she said, almost too softly. "I don't remember what we did last weekend." She repeated as though telling herself the second time. I felt uncomfortable, like I was overhearing an intimate conversation that I shouldn't but didn't want to give away that I was there, overhearing it.

"What do you mean Mom?" I asked, hoping she was just messing with me. But somehow I knew she wasn't.

"We went swimming with Little Bear, remember? And watched a movie, you said the actor was handsome." I laughed a little as I said it. She hadn't said handsome, she'd said *hot*. It was weird to think of mom looking at a man like I look at a man. She didn't seem to hear me. She continued.

"I worry myself sometimes. There are these blanks. Like I've been drinking, but you know I haven't. I don't feel the same anymore. I forget a lot, periods of time." She looked over at me.

Her voice caught. "I think I'm going to be one of those people who doesn't recognize my family when I'm old." She now looked like she was fighting back tears. Mom never cried.

"Oh, mom, stop it, you'll be fine. You've always been a little forgetful. Plus, you're young. Stop worrying about it." Again she seemed not to hear me. She rolled up the window and looked at me, waiting for me to take her cue. I did, my silent baby dropping pieces of wet doughnut onto my arms as I cranked the window shut. My ears seemed a mile away.

"The doctor says I'm showing signs of dementia." She paused. She wasn't joking. I was dizzy with a kick of adrenaline. I could feel my heart pounding under Little Bear.

"My confusion, memory loss, my moodiness. Don't say you haven't noticed." She took the cigarette I was offering her, trying not to let her see my hand was shaking. Moodiness yes. I had noticed. But I had just chalked it up to suddenly being responsible for a teenage mom and her baby.

"Mom?" She didn't let me ask my question.

"They say once it starts it can continue up to twenty-five years. I just wanted you to know. And so don't be mad for bringing you here. You know I love you. And Little Bear. I'm so happy he . . ." She stroked his face and looked at me fleetingly before forcing her eyes back to the road. "You shouldn't have him out of the car seat," she said.

I didn't know what to say so I didn't say anything. I thought of driving the yellow rusted truck myself, with only the wind beating its way around the cab. I could imagine the future only from movies I'd watched. In horror, I saw my mother vanish, her eyes empty and unrecognizing. I thought of taking care of her and our house echoing with another ghost. I thought of her smell disappearing from the sheets, the walls, the carpet. I thought of the dad I didn't know with smelly feet and jump rope hair. As the sun was going down I saw the sign: *crow indian reservation* it whispered. I clutched Little Bear tight as though he was about to slip away and he wriggled to get free of my grip, whimpering a little. We were eye level with the fields.

"We're here," Mom said.

NEIL UZZELL

Granddaddy

Everyone in town thought he was a lunatic, but he was just an alcoholic. He drove around in his sky blue Buick LeSabre with a .38 pistol next to him. When his emphysema came, the doctors told him he'd be hospitalized for the rest of his life. He responded by throwing off his gown and marching out of the intensive care unit completely nude.

At the age of sixty-five he had been forced to resign from the small town high school because he'd marched into the Superintendent's office drunk and told him what a "piss poor education system" he was running. Since it had been the tenth time in a series of drunken rants, the Superintendent had anticipated my grandfather's arrival with a tape recorder in the drawer of his desk.

The last night I saw him he sat in his favourite blue chair, his feet propped on the ottoman, a glass of whisky in one hand, and his prescription medication in the other.

"You're my favourite grandson, Cowboy." He told me.

"I'm your only grandson, sir."

The day he died, I took his shotgun into the backyard and fired it in the air until I ran out of shells.

Dog

My father bought me a German Shepard when I was a boy. He thought that every boy should have a dog, a companion to keep him company. When my father brought him home from the kennel, he built a pen in the backyard for it to sleep in. The feeding and shit shovelling responsibility was left to me. I woke up every morning at six o'clock and took care of the chore. We lived on old farmland littered with empty barns, trees whose branches reached into the middle of the yard, and a little pump house that looked like a face in the dark.

I woke up one winter morning in the dark, walked through the yard absentmindedly, fed the dog, and came back into the light of the porch to discover several swollen spiders crawling on my head. I screamed and flailed wildly until my father came outside and roared as I removed all of the spiders. The same afternoon he put a granddaddy long-legs down my shirt and told me to be a man about it.

I was somewhat reluctant to complete the chore afterwards. The barns looked like creatures of the night, and out of the corner of my eye the pump house's face contorted when I tried to go out and feed the dog. So, I just stood in the yard for several minutes each morning pretending I had fed it. I was awakened each night by howling, and in the morning the animal shuffled nervously around the pen. Once, I threw a chicken bone from several yards away and heard harsh thrashing, snarling, and crunching sounds. When my father ordered me to give the dog a bath, I told him I was afraid. He laughed, "That sounds like an excuse I'd have used." When I insisted, he threatened me with the belt, so I took my chances with the wild.

The dog looked mangy from the cage. He barked and paced up and down the pen. He froze when I lifted my hand to free him. When the door was opened, he tore through as if I might be teasing him and made a beeline for the woods. He stopped briefly at the pump house to turn and stare at me. Then darted into the woods and disappeared.

ALICE NOTLEY

Foundation

I don't comprehend how to be French or anything else
They say I'm an American; I am among us, with requisite facial
organs and stories on my skin. I can't seem to fall asleep
an ethos of an hour ago old as the dust of intention to love all debris

all this debris-covered quartier. How can I found us without screaming
The minister of the interior unlucidly arrests the tattered violets of the banlieus
For they sense there is nothing to do but wear their deepest purple cagoules
Who sees flowers among these configurations it isn't a movie, Jack
it's a moment of defiance and if you frame it you still can't invent our forms that
        leap in lightning streamers.

Inside myself I vandalize your comforting earnings
I want to be paid for my emotions, don't you? I want to
be paid for everything I've gone through. I want to steal your
respectability, and change the titles of all your poems to Inserts In an Ass.
You smell like someone who would leave a shattered dancer on the sidewalk to
        answer your cellphone
ancient wolf howls on the unconcerned marble steps. Boys we got in
to the University of Iceberg; our fathers and mothers are happy with frosted
        eyebrows and white lips.

Everyone will now enter the Chinese restaurant. I am allowed
only one dish, of fish paste and pale celery. Why do you get two?
Have you read this cretinous review, of last year's riots? We were the authors
of the violence, rocking ourselves to sleep. We are the gentle wheat
to be scythed later, growing near the train tracks

Two hundred kilometers an hour. Speed grazes us with its beauty
A human being stutters, and is unremembered after he leaves the screen.

My City

The nightmare of treason had recohered. Had come back, thrilling.
My apartment in the grand train station rendered me apart
as truly as if by mandate. It seems as if I've always lived here
It's a city of politics, manifs, bombs. I have plotted, myself,
to take over hearts and minds, because it's so easy; but I didn't
want the responsibility of tyranny. And I know pain
in a maiming fashion that will immobilize me when it's time
to do more than stare at your forehead, time to cut it open and
insert the story.

Consider me as both Antony and Caesar. And know that
the famous word "honorable" has been changed. To "formidable,"
no that's not it. "Horrible"—spelled W-H-O-R-E-A-B-L-E.
Women have betrayed themselves by evolving vaginas:
they "selected for" those organs. By some theorists it is propounded
that one's wishes prior to conception, carried backwards
from a future of perverse reasoning and scrolled-out
motivation, are at work. Caesar asked to be delivered by Caesarian.

I come to bury Caesar not to praise him. But I have
betrayed Brutus and Cassius, who plotted against me
in full train station light. In my city. No
woman has a city. I lower my blinds—so I can't
see them through the window or they can't see me?
I may have left fingerprints as the betrayer,
I betray by knowing they would betray:
I shouldn't know that our country is ruled by forces secret

from those who contain them. But I am so apart how could I
be instrumental in exposing your plot to murder me?

In the poetics of our times, many have paid attention
to the treason of choosing one word over another.
I walk amid the finally shattered glass
broken to articulate my reasonable but passionate
speeches to you who conspire against my power.
The man who tried to pick me up at the Gare de l'Est yesterday
was shorter than I, quite ugly. He asked for directions, then said
Viens avec moi. I have passed a lifetime unable to
move freely, think without interruption, or be friendly. Freedom
of thought, motion, impulse remains unacceptable.
I want to found a city of free minds mingling. Are there no free minds
except for mine?

Story to the river-2

I am provoked by realism's cellphone to call up the Minister of the Interior
I need my interior oxygenated, more relaxed. Excellent, he breathes, I can expel
the illegal invaders of yourself, Madame; I have calculated
you need to get rid of tens of thousands pretending to be light, when factually
our deft economy selects urban grisaille as Soul.

But Monsieur I want you to leave me; I need an undishevelled
emptiness within. I seek amatory absence, I later tell the Seine
not any betterment; he thinks because I'm white I'm not an immigrant
having arrived fourteen years ago collapsed feeding tube
on the floor, for no good reason. Who needs a whore-
driven reason? That's the job of the clown-fuck philosophe

mine is to sing this preposterous animal tongue I was born in.
A youth has blown snot out all over his head, in the shape
of our noble continent: a green-beige topological map.
He must symbolize me; my interior's now free, exteriorized expat.

A lot of people must have come here only to embroider
thrilling arteries with companionable cars, their colours and auditory
tones. Really, you have to want to buy one. This city
has everything; I am a phantom. I once dreamt of a pale
horse who spoke and told me Death was an articulate beauty,
but didn't mean Death as we think of it for he wasn't dead.

Perhaps we have not thought of anything.
You escort to your borders a form of courage; how brave to come alone,
without money or flag. *Vous êtes courageuse*, someone said to me,
because I had continued to live. This is my story, River,
its details are new locations of my wrathful and graceful hours
as I walk casually beside you without appointment or compliance.

In the truth room

Can we even move without each other
the light connecting us or is that what we are
I saw zipped-up tissue fall open
but the bloody-lipped cartoon face was mine.

In the truth room our own hands put him together
our dishes and sacraments and sentences gone to wisps
if we made me, can we live with that
I'm trying to get to you though you're always there
all of you, and the light pouring out of my throat is you, too.

It's humorous that you can't even call me up
because my language is wrong. These configurations
cross the gangplank collapsing ashore. Where did we come
from? Nowhere. "Tell them we're like infinite twins"
comes to me. Where does it come from nowhere
I may look like that but that's not me

"I could find you again if I wanted, if I wanted you"
if I am you how can I want that "immigrant or pilgrim"
"very easy for you" and division is created. I don't approve
of your flicker light words. How do we speak
oh the apparatus, isn't that interesting

I found that I was dappled, covered with shadow.
Someone walks by, because the legs go—will you
cover for me when I'm in trouble; gearing
up for a future. If I leave this moment

I wanted to put things in it. Do I have to;
points of connection. Words are enough—we
don't need anything else. All we have in the truth room
are light and some words. Then the tissue
knits back together, zips up fast.

Diary entry

If you try to obliterate your celebrated ego, others will bolster it with rich chains filled with the cushioning fluid they put in sneakers. Is the dead gay artist still gay? The imitators have made him wear their imitations, which are glossy and require long doggy ears. He doesn't seem to mind, and I say I find the finish rather beautiful, in the inevitable way you're appropriated by starlets whose muted talents keep a virginal electricity in circulation. He's so cute.

You are puncturing me with desire, I mean you, Review; the *moi* floated back through the racy trees in the form of ancient flesh-packed calendars, the smell of confessional poverty, anti-terrorist readings of a facial expression. For we are in the new time, bathing our subconscious in the fumes from sado-masochistic heir in his hideaway no grace notes; *I* can't have a rendezvous.

The woman appeared, from thousands of miles away, in the little living room. She could do this now since she was very old; her grand-daughter and some stray baby were there too. The point was to soften me up for a visit from someone who really wasn't there, a different dead man, who informed me I was now the leader of a lot of spirits. This century is really crazy with hundreds of souls piled on my exams so I can't take them, I can only be here trying to divine Here's wishes, before it mineralizes.

I would like to lead you back to your ego-husks; they are comfortable and litup. Inside, the light, inexhaustible, never waivers, so you can see each other, who never had any publicity. I watch the landscape, waiting for the wilderness to walk towards me; at first a map but then at least one real tree, a little pulled in towards itself as if by a hairnet, but green three-dimensional and projected towards me. It seemed to move.

We are not examples and have no slogans. We are extinct in conventional time and don't have to be jealous; once fucked by ecstasy on the fire exit stairs, always fucked by ecstasy on the fire exit stairs. Proper nutrition is not an issue, nor medication, nor the possibility of contempt. We don't have to take vows or keep hours. Rip down the boring memorial: it gives us a headache.

The Beaded Horse

A small white horse from another planet wishes to talk to me.
It is only a few inches in length. Its skin is composed of white beads
White-beaded it speaks, hesitantly, in English
It has vocal chords. It has a pink mouth and tongue.
Heavenly seedpearls for horsehair? Try not to reach a rationale

Only to myself on welfare and in public: for I came to you
when you least expected new knowledge in your candled reality,
frying squash blossoms dipped in batter, on the courthouse lawn.
Leave this town. Oh, one cannot go back on a planetary promise.

You never promised the earth your skeleton, it assumes it
I hate this cajoling universe, these passionate black-winged moths
telling my eyes to perceive nothing but their sisterly claws.

Can you find the Law in this town? An infidel possesses my voice.
Who are they to degrade me, they so easily imagined?
Only a dream could make them be of interest.

My sister the Fury had told me, I couldn't get over heartbeat.
Or break she said heat of the orange rift, chimera of our alphabet
The girls fly screaming above the moving walkway.
Listen to the horsie—too white. You're painting the walls of heaven
too white, says the African dropping his teacup I catch it

Where are you going? Anyone? Stop telling me things, staging events,
trying to focus on agreement, in our corner of this constriction,
room of no landscape and filthy apron. This is what I have against heaven.

The desert of minutes remembers us well, so do We have to?
The people whose care was enslavement. Your drug addiction
in my kitchen? A haunting tenant plots to take over
a street gang in this afterlife; and her passivity and nicer still, his manicure
flashes dutifully across the skies. I took a bullet for you.
We are the reminiscing convicts—One way or another, one would kill

that was our ideal. Our desperation, our incarnate bread.
Some people are called perverse for the audience's pleasure.
I just don't want to be here, though you have lovely qualities.
The horse isn't of this nature, being magical
struggling to speak to us; hasn't it come from its own revolutionary land?

The superior man had said, Look at these white walls we've painted.
       I can't stay, I said,
I have a problem. Effects, he said. Yes, effects. Personal
and consequential. But we'll meet in the living room again, to look
at the flawless drawings. I awoke and remembered my own priceless

artwork was ruined. Where grace overdue doubts you
generations of satellites clank above the trees, bringing satisfaction
       from the vacuous regions
Out of the dark confinement, out of the more moneyed arts.

The horse's tiny tongue is working again
Twisted to shape you, tulip of assignment. It could be about
heroin or shamanism. I could sing your ravenous adherences
The woman was cut into three pieces, accompanied by successful yields,
retrieval of indulgences, and a movie star's penchant for charity.

Horse says they always promise to make it up to you in other ways.
For example as you grow old they'll wipe your dribble with a tissue.
I speak as someone having trouble with a foreign language—Look
the girls are back! The Furies divebomb us shrieking.

You must accompany me to complete beauty.
Don't return to the ugly projects, mount their stairs—
elevator danger. Heaven has always been characterized
by the gap between the rich and the poor. *They*
know how to rise. The oligarchs *mean* to be nice.
These are the figures of diction and the figures of thought.

An open-minded bird erupts from my forehead; we are going away
from lustful reversals and all «man» has ever held dear. What's there?
The same gibberish, customs, drugs? No way
It's where the Law is clear. The silver malevolence
streaming down on the ocean was projected by realism, riches, psychic
vibrations of hierarchy. I am going for your heart.

I had wanted out but I kept returning for my purse, I tell the
horse, it contains my effects—have I left them this time?
Riding you away from the countries of age, are we the travelling souls
I've got to get there, do I need my passport,
my name, and everything I've done, to myself and everyone?

No, says the horse, not now, and No
ancient foibles, diaries, roulette, Greek drama. Orange malicious boulevard
a diet of flames reflected on my white beads'
cadenzas: Hell brought us here. There was nothing to learn
by following rules: this is the Law. Clamorous beauty of courage

Sunflowers everywhere clotted black centres. The tremors
of your legs have ceased. No fear now, there was so much of it.
Those who are contrary to the old empire, you who hated have arrived.

Heal more than one. We've arrived here with nothing,
not even what we thought of us. We are more deadly and savage,
more exalted than they've ever known;
Here we are the City, that indelicate miracle
not your manners or your children

did you really think you knew how to organize us
body after body, our deaths twisting in the wind? Here, in
our city, we don't please anyone.

Out of the orange snow and the legality of disaffection; out of the
sombre, broken crescent, and the overdue soul; out of the streaming forelock
from our omniscient minds: this liquid dimension has awakened
out of barbary and stretchers.

JOHN BERGER

Le Passeur/The Guide Across Frontiers

Ken was born in New Zealand and died there. I sit on the bench opposite him. This man, sixty years ago, shared with me what he knew, although he never told me how he learnt what he knew. He never spoke about his childhood or his parents. I had the impression he left New Zealand for Europe when he was young, before he was twenty. Were his parents rich or poor? Maybe it makes as little sense to ask that question of him as it would of the people in this market at this moment.

Distances never daunted him. Wellington, New Zealand, Paris, New York, the Bayswater Road, London, Norway, Spain, and at some moment, I think, Burma or India. He earned his living, variously, as a journalist, a schoolteacher, a dance instructor, an extra in films, a gigolo, a bookseller without a shop, a cricket umpire. Maybe some of what I'm saying is false, yet it is my way of making a portrait of him for myself as he sits in front of me in the Place Nowy. In Paris he drew cartoons for a newspaper, of this I am certain. I remember distinctly the kind of toothbrushes he liked—ones with extra long handles, and I remember the size of shoe he took—an eleven.

From the bag slung over my shoulder I take out a sketchbook, for I want to show him a drawing I made yesterday from Leonardo's *Lady with an Ermine* in the Czartoryski Museum. He studies it, his heavy glasses slipping a little down his nose.

Pas mal! Yet isn't she too upright? Isn't she in fact leaning more as she takes the corner?

On hearing him speak in this way, which is so indisputably his, my love for him comes back: my love for his journeys; for his appetites, which he set out to satisfy and never suppressed; for his weariness; for his sad curiosity.

A little too upright, he repeats. Never mind, every copy has to change something, doesn't it?

My love for his lack of illusions comes back too. Without illusions, he avoided disillusionment.

When I first met him I was eleven and he forty. For the next six or seven years he was the most influential person in my life. It was with him that I learnt to cross frontiers. In French there is the word *passeur*—often translated as ferryman or smuggler. Yet there is also in the word the connotation of guide, and something of the mountains. He was my *passeur*.

Ken flips backwards through the sketchbook. He had deft fingers and could palm cards skilfully. He tried to teach me Find the Lady: *You can always make money with that!* he said. Now he puts a finger between two pages and stops

Another copy? Antonello da Messina?

Dead Christ Supported by an Angel, I say.

I never saw it, only in reproduction. If I could have chosen to have my portrait painted by any artist in history, I'd have chosen him, he says. Antonello. He painted like he was printing words. Everything he painted had that kind of coherence and authority, and it was during his lifetime that the first printing presses were invented.

He looks down again at the sketchbook.

Not a trace of pity on the angel's face or in his hands, he says, only tenderness. You've caught that tenderness, but not the gravity, the gravity of the first printed words. That's gone for good.

I did it last year in the Prado. Until the guards came to chuck me out.

Anyone has the right to draw there, no?

Yes, but not to sit on the floor.

Then why didn't you draw standing up!

When Ken says this in the Place Nowy, I see him, tall, stooped, standing on the edge of a cliff making a sketch of the sea. Near Brighton, the summer of 1939. He always carried in his pocket a large black graphite pencil called a Black Prince, which, instead of being round, was rectangular like a carpenter's pencil.

I'm too old now, I tell him, to draw for a long time standing up.

He puts down the sketchbook abruptly without glancing at me. He abhorred self-pity. The weakness, he said, of many intellectuals. Avoid it! This was the only moral imperative he ever imparted to me.

Néanmoins! French words cropped up in his sentences not out of affectation but because the years he had lived in Paris before coming to London and the Bayswater Road, were the happiest of his life. It was for the same reason that he sometimes wore a black beret.

I met him in 1937. He was a replacement teacher in the lunatic boarding school to which I had been bundled. In front of the school assembly—fifty bare-kneed, cowed boys, each trying to find, unaided, a sense to life—the apoplectic headmaster threw a dining-room chair at the Latin teacher and Ken, who happened to be between them, caught it with one hand in mid-flight. This is how I first noticed him. He set the chair down on the podium, put his feet up on it, and the boss continued to harangue.

In the final day of that same term I invited him to a caravan my parents had on a beach near Selsea Bill in Sussex. Why not? he said. And he came for a week

My mother quickly recognized that Ken belonged to what for her was the special category of "people who loved Paris."

Watching the three of us playing quoits on the sand, she foresaw, I'm sure, that the *passeur* was going to take me a long way away and, at the same time, she didn't doubt, I'm equally sure, that, give or take a little, I was capable of looking after myself. Consequently, she offered on Monday, Wash Day, to launder and iron his clothes, and Ken bought her a bottle of Dubonnet.

I accompanied Ken to bars and, although I was under age, nobody ever objected. Not on account of my size or looks, but on account of my certainty. Don't look back, he told me, don't doubt for a moment, just be surer of yourself than they are.

Once, another drinker started swearing at me—telling me to get my bloody mouth out of his sight—and I suddenly broke down. Ken put his arm round me and took me straight out into the street. There were no lights. This was in wartime

London. We walked a long way in silence. If you have to cry, he said, and sometimes you can't help it, if you have to cry, cry afterwards, never during! Remember this. Unless you're with those who love you, only those who love you, and in that case you're already lucky for there are never many who love you—if you're with them, you can cry during. Otherwise you cry afterwards.

All the games he taught me, he played well. Except for his short-sightedness (suddenly it occurs to me, as I write, that all the people I have loved and still love were or are short-sighted), except for his short-sightedness, he moved like an athlete. A similar poise.

Not me. I was clumsy, over-hasty, cowardly, with almost no poise. I had something else though. A kind of determination, which, given my age, was startling. I would wager all! And for the energy of that rashness, he overlooked the rest. And the gift of his love was the gift of sharing with me what he knew, almost everything he knew, irrespective of my age or his.

For such a gift to be possible the giver and receiver need to be equal, and we, strange, incongruous pair that we were, became equal. Probably neither of us understood how this happened. Now we do. We were foreseeing this moment; we were equal then as we are equal now in the Place Nowy. We foresaw my being an old man and his being dead, and this allowed us to be equal.

He puts his long hand around the can of beer on the table and clinks it against mine.

Whenever possible, he preferred gestures to spoken words. Perhaps as a result of his respect for silent written words. He must have studied in libraries, yet for him the immediate place for a book was a raincoat pocket. And the books he pulled out of that pocket!

He did not hand them to me directly. He said the name of the author, he pronounced the title, and he placed the book on the corner of the mantelpiece in his bed-sitting room. Sometimes there were several, one on top of the other, so that I might choose. George Orwell. *Down and Out in Paris and London*. Marcel

Proust. *Swann's Way.* Katherine Mansfield. *The Garden Party.* Laurence Sterne. *The Life and Opinions of Tristam Shandy.* Henry Miller. *Tropic of Cancer.* Neither of us, for different reasons, believed in literary explanations. I never once asked him about what I failed to understand. He never referred to what, given my age and experience, I might find difficult to grasp in these books. Sir Frederick Treves. *The Elephant Man and Other Reminiscences.* James Joyce. *Ulysses.* (An English edition published in Paris.) There was a tacit understanding between us that we learn—or try to learn—how to live partly from books. The learning begins with looking at our first illustrated alphabet, and goes on until we die. Oscar Wilde. *De Profundis.* St. John of the Cross.

When I gave a book back, I felt closer to him, because I knew a little more of what he had read during his long life. Books converged us. Often one book led to another. After George Orwell's *Down and Out in Paris and London,* I wanted to read *Homage to Catalonia.*

Ken was the first person to talk to me about the Spanish Civil War. Open wounds, he said. Nothing can staunch them. I had never heard the word *staunch* pronounced out loud before. We were at that moment playing billiards in a bar. Don't forget to chalk the cue, he added.

He read to me in Spanish a poem by Garcia Lorca, who had been shot four years earlier, and when he translated it, I believed in my fourteen-year-old mind that I knew—except for a few details—what life was about and what had to be risked! Perhaps I told him so, or perhaps some other rashness of mine provoked him, for I remember him saying: Check out the details! Check them out first not last!

He said this with a note of regret as if somewhere, somehow, he himself had made a mistake about details that he regretted. No, I'm wrong. He was a man who regretted nothing. A mistake for which he had had to pay the price. During his life he paid the price for many things he didn't regret.

EDDY BELLEVILLE

Poem

It's down by the river
   that Paris comes back to me.

The colour of sky at a distance

sluicing between islands

tugs at the
mossy-lunged root.

Forest mouths
smack silty lips
and drink in the ancient
cloud burst,

rolling in marbles

from the duck's back
through the hands of the skipping stone bridges

and beyond,
to where rippling pilgrims
patter the sun.

Poem

A strawman, sweet as berries,

—that's how I set you up.

But you rose

over the lamplight,

eyes black as buttons

and fiddlier

fastened to mine

lip and brow curled

white horses

cresting

the wave,

and in my sunny contempt

made lemonade and hay.

JONATHAN HAMRICK

Among Other Things

It was a heavy old-fashioned mirror with rococo flourishes, faded and oxidized, that the man carried down some street, or rather, some *rue*. I was in a *laverie,* waiting for my clothes to dry, looking at the man through the window, and so maybe I should have known which *rue*, but I didn't, or I don't remember. The mirror was full-length and free-standing, with small feet attached to a frame from which the mirror could swivel. It was with great and obvious effort that the man kept the feet from scraping the concrete. Scrapes were inevitable, though, and with each one he cursed loudly, or did something that seemed like cursing. I couldn't tell because I couldn't understand him. A cigarette dangled from his mouth. He was fat, sweating, and his shirt was untucked and mostly unbuttoned.

I didn't help the man. I spent a few seconds thinking about what heroic story he would tell his fat wife or mother (probably it was for his mother) about how he got this ugly mirror, a thing he hated but that he thought would please this woman whose sadness was all but implacable. His story would have something to do with a dirty gaunt man with foul teeth and a short, razor-sharp beard. The man, despite his thinness, would be obviously strong in the way snakes are. The gaunt man would be standing before the mirror, not admiring himself in it, but tilting it so it would reflect the sun in just the right way to catch the eye of any passersby. It wasn't ideal if it temporarily blinded them, but if it happened, well, he couldn't avoid it.

The gaunt man owned a shop, where he had many items for sale: picture frames, women's gloves, baskets, small pots of no discernable use, two pairs of old-fashioned boxing gloves, and other things. The mirror was something he'd won in a card game, a bet he'd accepted for no other reason than to take the very last of another man's possessions, to leave a man with nothing.

He'd fallen before for this trick of winning what someone else wanted more than anything to lose, though he hadn't understood that it was a trick, rather than a cheat, until now, with the mirror. He'd won radios that looked new but didn't work, vases held together with flimsy but invisible glue, a box of fake gold rings. He'd thrown these things away, or broken them, smashed them against a sidewalk or a wall, and promised he'd harm the man that had cheated him.

With the mirror it was different. He knew he'd been tricked when he tried to carry the thing down the street. It was impossible to hold the mirror and move at the same time. The mirror swiveled too freely in its frame. It swung as he stepped and hit him sharply in the shin. He adjusted it, but overcompensated, and the mirror swung downward and smacked his forehead, opening a cut that he didn't notice until a few steps later, when he expected to wipe sweat from his eye but found blood instead.

And yet, for all this, he didn't want the mirror to break. He even decided he'd fix it so it wouldn't swing so wildly. This wasn't superstition, but rather that he felt some strange attachment to the mirror, even though he hated it and hated himself for taking such a burden on himself in the interest of destroying someone else. Yet, he had won it, hadn't he? Didn't that count for something? He wanted to get it to his shop. Even now, as he carried it, he imagined himself displaying it outside, on the sidewalk, during the day, and tilting it so that the sun struck it just right.

When the fat man came and stood before the mirror, the gaunt man knew he would take it, regardless of the price. And the gaunt man, call him Lucien, realized that he could part with the mirror, and that, at the same time, he didn't want to take the fat man's money, though he knew he could name his price. Call the fat man Laurent. But what price could he name? The mirror was all but worthless. It had value to Lucien only insofar as he had acquired it, and then worked miserably to carry it to his shop. He'd suffered a minor injury because of it. But what value did that give it?

It was clear from the way Laurent, the fat man, regarded the mirror that he would have it, and that he wouldn't, for any reason, give it up. Lucien was a good salesman, with a great deal of experience selling things people didn't want or wanted but didn't understand why.

"It's interesting, isn't it," Lucien, his French calm and idiomatic, said to Laurent. He held out a pack of cigarettes.

"What's interesting?" said Laurent, skittish, unaware of the pack, but catching a look at himself and Lucien in the mirror: two men that couldn't have looked more different.

"That mirror," lighting his own cigarette, then pointing it at the mirror.

Now Laurent noticed the offered pack, but only after it had disappeared with the hand holding it to Lucien's side. Was it too late?

It wasn't too late. Lucien, noticing Laurent's interest—he had an eye for this— offered the pack again. Laurent took a cigarette, and let Lucien light it.

"That mirror," said Lucien, gesturing theatrically, as if trying to make the Lucien in the mirror look as genuine as possible. "That mirror is priceless."

"Priceless?"

"It has no price."

"It's not for sale?"

"I didn't say that."

In a sense, this conversation could have happened anywhere. There are always things to be bought and sold in any place, and there are always things without prices, though often people never know about those things.

Yet, even if there was an obviously universal quality to the exchange, there was also no denying its particularity: that it took place in a part of Paris, France near Père Lachaise and Place de la Nation, between a gaunt man named Lucien and a fat man named Laurent. Their desires and fears were shaped by these facts, among others, including that both men were, in fact, born very near the spot where the conversation took place. And yet, Paris, France? A place among many. One place among many named Paris, in fact. In the United States alone there are cities in Arkansas, Idaho, Illinois, Kentucky, Maine, Michigan, Missouri, New York, Ohio, Pennsylvania, Tennessee, Texas, and Virginia called Paris. This is related to how the letters in "Paris France" make those words, but also many others.

Pecan Friars, Fracas Ripen, and Farce Sprain are three of the thousands of other possible combinations.

Lucien went on:

"The fact is, even if it has no price, I still want you to have it."

No response from Laurent, though he did smoke more slowly.

"But I'm in business. You understand. It's hard to say what it's worth to you, of course, since it's hard to say what it's worth to me."

"You'd like to trade values," Laurent, throwing down his cigarette, becoming more alert.

"Ordinarily, yes."

It wasn't clear to Laurent what Lucien was up to. He took tobacco and papers from his pocket and rolled a cigarette, slowly, paying close attention to it. He understood something about the peripheral gestures and feints important to business deals.

"The fact is," Lucien went on. "I can't sell it. I can't. When I say it's priceless," and he waved his cigarette, letting this uninterpretable gesture finish his thought.

"So what would you like to have for it?" Laurent's cigarette was now rolled, and he lit it with his own lighter.

This was a good question, and one whose answer Lucien had been considering from the moment he saw Laurent admiring the mirror. It had to be something credible, the exchange, and yet something Laurent couldn't fail to provide. This was important. Lucien was convinced that the mirror was priceless, and also that he hated it and yet was also attached to it. He was convinced that the fat man, Laurent, was also attached to it and that he should have it. These principles and convictions were in conflict, but it didn't make any sense not to hold them.

"Chess," Lucien said finally.

"Chess?"

"I have a board in there somewhere." Lucien disappeared into his shop.

Laurent, as it happened, was a good chess player. He had, when he was younger, beaten a man who would go on to be recognized as one of the world's best players. It was at a bar near Belleville. Laurent was drinking his beer quietly, enjoying the solitude of the din, when, seemingly from nowhere, a voice said, in a foreign accent, maybe an English or an American accent:

"Anybody that beats me at chess, I buy two beers for him, and give two-hundred Francs. Any comers?"

Laurent played chess at a small club, and could consistently beat the other members. He needed a suitable opponent. He could use the beer, too, and the money. So he accepted the challenge.

The game took three hours, during which neither man looked the other in the eye. Laurent was white, and played a King's Indian Attack, a system he'd never used before. Early on, he was sure he'd lose. Shortly after setting up the attack, the other man easily penetrated into his half of the board.

Laurent stared at the board for a full twenty minutes at one point before he saw in his mind an extraordinarily long and counterintuitive series of moves that, if played out properly, would give him a convincing, if exhausting, victory. This wasn't the first time he'd had such an experience. Over the course of many games, he'd learned he was a cagey strategist, capable of developing a bleak middle game into a surprising victory.

He ended up sacrificing his queen and a bishop to advance the pawns on his queenside, the side left vulnerable by the King's Indian Attack. Even after Laurent had promoted a pawn to queen, he needed fourteen moves to achieve checkmate. He counted them off in his head, because he'd already seen them.

It was agonizing for his opponent. Laurent could tell by the way the man handled his pieces that he understood, after a certain point, that Laurent was completely in control, and that the game had proceeded exactly according to his plan.

The man gathered his board and pieces and left the bar without paying Laurent.

Laurent continued to play his opponents at the club, but was quickly bored. With no adequate challengers, he quit playing entirely.

Years later, he saw in the newspaper an obituary with a picture of his opponent. He was American. The obituary said the man had won the world championship only a year after the day he'd lost to Laurent. He had been found dead. Suicide, apparently.

Laurent told himself it was only luck that led him to beat the man. Only luck. When he discovered, years later, that he could play chess against computer programs on the Internet, he refused. He wouldn't try his luck again.

Now, he was sure the gaunt man, Lucien, was not only a good player, and not only in practice, but eager for an opponent. He was sure Lucien had been looking for a chance not only to play a game, but to torture another man's desires. What would he, Lucien, the gaunt man, want in exchange for his victory? Or, if Laurent did win the mirror, what would he lose by winning it? And, of course, what about the game itself? What if Laurent lost this game? What if he won? What would either mean to his life, his future?

Chess wasn't possible. He couldn't win playing chess.

It was at this moment that Laurent noticed the old-fashioned boxing gloves in Lucien's window. He'd never had a fight in his life.

When Lucien appeared with the board and pieces, Laurent lied: "Chess isn't my game really. I've wondered about putting on the gloves again, though, what it would take . . ." He gestured at the old, tough gloves.

"Those?"

And now Lucien wondered. He had never played chess in his life. In fact, he hardly knew how the pieces moved. And yet, did this fat man think that, just because he'd suggested a game of chess, he couldn't, or wouldn't, fight? More important than giving the mirror away, he saw now, had been to see if there was a man that would play for it, that would wager on its pricelessness. And now? Was it not clear that those gloves had once belonged to him? That he had used them well? And that they were as priceless and as undesirable as this mirror?

"Boxing is your game?"

They would fight in the small concrete court behind Lucien's shop. The men agreed to three one-minute rounds to start. Lucien brought an old alarm clock from his shop to keep time. Yet, neither man could set the clock with his gloved hands. It was, in fact, difficult enough for the men to tie, with their teeth, their second gloves.

Lucien proposed a solution:

"I understand," he said. "I understand you want to give that mirror away to your wife or your mother or your sister and say you won it in a fight. So here's the deal. I hit you once, hard enough to blacken your eye, and you take the mirror. Then you can say anything you like."

Laurent, too shy to acknowledge that this was, truly, what he'd had in mind, said nothing. But, his jaw was clenched. Lucien could see that.

The result of the punch was better than a black eye. It was a large bruise to the side of the eye, between the corner of the eye and the temple, and a shallow but obvious cut below the eye. It hurt, yes, but it was a game: childlike, even nostalgic. Lucien gave Laurent the mirror, as well as a cigarette and a shot of whiskey.

And what Laurent told his fat mother was: "An old gaunt man was standing outside his shop, smoking. I was on the other side of the street, having a smoke myself. Then, out of nowhere, three young men set upon the shopkeeper. Did he owe them money? Were they just looking for trouble? It didn't matter. I ran over and threw one of them off. Then one caught me in the eye, gave me this. I hit him back. By now, the old man had recovered himself, and the kids were confused. He must have been an old fighter, because he went at one kid like an old fighter would, an old fighter that wants to prove to some kids he's not old. And then I took care of the one that hit me. By now, the first one I'd knocked down had gotten scared and run away. His friends followed. The old man was tough. He'd taken a good punch, right in the eye, much worse than what I've got here. I was lucky, he was tough. Anyway, he said he'd give me anything, and when I tried to walk away with only his thanks, he insisted I take something. He was a tough guy, the kind that could turn on you. So I took this mirror. I knew how you'd like it . . ."

When the man had passed out of my sight, a young woman came into the *laverie*. My clothes were still drying. Eight minutes to go. I didn't want to look at her, but I could tell she was confused by the *laverie*. And, from the corner of my eye, I could tell she was trying to get my attention. I did all I could to ignore her. Finally, she said, "*Excusez-moi?*" and then something I couldn't understand but that I knew meant, "How do you work things here in this *laverie*?"

I told her the truth, "*Je ne parle pas français.*" That was the truth, despite my better than adequate accent.

She persisted, though. She talked in French, looked at me intently, gestured at the various machines, the one that took your money and started the washers and dryers, and at the washers and dryers themselves. There were instructions posted, in French, on the walls. I couldn't read them, but I could figure out how to use the machines. She couldn't figure out the machines, but she knew French. We were the only ones in the *laverie*.

So, what could we do but stumble through it? She put all her clothes, whites and colours, into a machine. Then she realized she could separate them, and use two machines, but that she'd have to pay for two machines. She didn't mind. She moved the whites to another machine. We agreed on temperatures for each load. Hot water, *eau chaude*, for the whites, and cold water, *eau froide*, for the colours. With my help, she bought a small packet of powdered detergent and loaded some into each machine.

Then she went to insert her money. *Deux machines. Introduire argent, monnaie, neuf euros.* I went to my dryer. Three minutes left. The clothes were still damp. They'd need another cycle. Still, I gathered them into my bag and, without saying a word to the woman, left the *laverie*. I went in the direction of the man with the mirror, but I didn't see him.

The situation, it seems, in which the mute is forced to lead the blind ends when the mute sees there's nothing to keep him from escaping.

BARBARA BECK

Travel: Border

Fantasies planted at random along the fence so-called back yard. one hand illegal, the other shows her full age. after northern winter she crosses the line under lights, sizzle of frying insects. voluptuous vibrato. the humming exacts travellers, shuts off the smuggle. any finger she touches without a word exchanged: handles, knobs, small change. considering the slightest thermal bridge is a flaw in insulation, gaping overture. imagine about one another never used up combinations. possible plenitudes equal double negative. cheap course of thought for a paltry otherness. knows about the likes of taxi drivers. the most disparate shame flowers golden yellow by the forced roadside. what could take place broken into unimportant parts. identify a head hers though not entirely. the alteration near the surface. there's little to do, why not what she positively wants, trade places even. stay as long as it takes, look neither rich nor strange.

Barbara Beck

Travel: Hospitality

Breezily in the village courting and coupling lots of jokes that she is such a free agent among chickens and grubby vegetables. even when nothing happens clings to sequence. a skinny woman's demeanour. small points of light are pilfered, the interpreter streaks off. her many introductions mixed together make all sorts after dark as she soon sees on the terrible roads. she wants to pop in and out of danger, sit single companionable on the ground. fly-infested openings and closings. there are zero vehicles going that way try again in the morning good night. can waiting be returned unassuaged like so many curious glances, other than leaving people poorer. or an inaction without perfectibility or known worth. time spent holding out a gift of fall-back candy as if to mimic fertility. all one afternoon she sleeps through the manioc pounding, the shriek of hens. in her edgeless dream a person offers a paying ride and she can't say no no not stranded enough for that.

DAVID ESO

The Lesser-Known Miracles of Jesus Christ

I.

on his 32nd day in the desert,
Jesus plunged an empty hand below the burning surface
& brought forth a glass jar full of sand.

giving the grains therein a bleary-brained stare,
only himself was heard to say
"Behold! Here is my synod!"

II.

elaborating upon an earlier performance
(some say surpassing),
halfway through the Last Supper
with a wave of his hand,
Jesus changed the Merlot
into Pinot Gris.

III.

Christian tradition has it that Jesus preached
in the synagogue as a preteen;
the Koran records the miracle
of the Christ child speaking from the manger;
some early drafts of the Book of Mormon, sadly lost,
reported baby Jesus suckling the Virgin and attendant livestock.

ALBERTO RIGETTINI

Last bath in Malaga

Like a snap of the tongue,
first drop.
Second,
as I emerge from the water.

I am water,
while another pearl
gently explodes on my forehead,
I've just felt another one
through my lips.

It's my ping pong
and I'm back into water,
sliding on my back,
a floating cross,
I sip and receive them on my face.

My last bath in Malaga
my last embrace to the wave
the water is flourishing,
touching me
where I'm naked.

I see the coast from here
calling its autumn
her palms waving
and tickling.
Sunset has never been so glad to see me.

Alberto Rigettini

Drops into irises
coming closer to the shore,
it's rain,
it's rain,
with a nestling's voice,
every last day is a day of love.

It's rain.
Waiters are running down
to collect the tables
waiters are running up
chiringuitos becoming shelters
and their bamboo waxier,

a teardrop on my cheek
a pinpoint on my chest
                and a thirst
water is tasting water
water is kissing water
water is falling in love
again   with water

In my last swim in Malaga
I don't want to emerge
and get dry out of here

now that everyone is running
now that my heart is sloshing its truth
now that I already have
a ticket to Italy.

When you sleep and your flower reposes

When you sleep and your flower reposes
as the shadow gets rich
imagination still sees

your feet are puppies now dozy
after playing so much
at chasing each other

when the colours ease their resistance

and everything aligns with blue

you sleep smooth, your heart smooth,
you donate peace to the room
and silence to the whole boulevard,

the only fear still ruffling breath
the only haste for the eyes to see is
a moment, in a moment
or another, you might wake up.

JESSICA MALCOMSON

I'll neologize you, baby

They are lovers, of a kind. They have sex, copiously, violently, in all sorts of fun and interesting ways. The other day, when he came in—they weren't in a roman-tic/sexual place, emotionally, either of them, but he still kissed her hello in front of everyone—proper, mouth-tongue kiss, not just *bises*. When they're together, out in the real world, they hold hands, or walk with their arms around each other. They kiss (and do a number of other things) in public. Whenever they meet amongst friends, each of them immediately seeks out the other. But—*but*, they both understand, this isn't a "re*l*ationship" in the way others understand the word: each of them is free to do what—and whom—they choose, with no judgment from the other one, no commitment, no obligations, no promises—no love.

She once described him as a sort of fuck buddy. But it goes beyond *that*, too. It's definitely not any kind of booty call arrangement, though they do call and arrange to meet, knowing they will end up having sex. Although, they don't always—she strains to remember. They have, every time they've seen each other, since that first time, but then, they've spent days together without having sex, and they don't generally leap straight into bed as soon as they meet.

Once, in fact—feels like forever ago, now. It was after several days together. Her place. Both excru*ci*atingly sober. Talking—playing word games. Neither of them had a lighter, so they were forced to light their cigarettes from the stovetop. Whenever they got up to do so, they sat back down a little closer together, gradu-ally moving towards the inevitable. Then—holding hands. Arms, legs, around each other. Soon, they're no longer sitting, but lying entangled on her bed.

Suddenly—he shifts position, blinks, shakes his head—trying to clear it. "Uh, do you mind if, tonight—we just cuddle?"

That shocked her. (Congratulations, she will think later. Not very easy to do.) She sits up suddenly—she always sits up properly for serious conversations, like people who have to put their glasses on in order to think—and stares at him. "You're joking."

"It's so del*i*cious just to hold you." He surfaces briefly from his reverie. "And, I'm *exhausted*. Barely slept last night. We haven't had a drink in *two days*."

"That's hardly an excuse. In fact, that's precisely *why* we have to find other—forms of stimulation." She sighs. Part of his appeal is his ability to frustrate her. He can be such a—what's the feminine version of prick-tease? Cunt-tease?

But, looking at him—such vulnerability now. And those eyes. Damn, his eyes. "Fine." Resigned. "Just—don't scare me like that again." Smiling. "Thought you were getting romantic in your old age." He's only a few years older than her, but she never lets him forget it.

He laughs—at her? At the idea of romance, between them? They stay there, just—she rejects the word "cuddling" Holding each other. *Being*, together. And then, of course, they have sex anyway. As he unzips, she mocks him. "Thought you were too tired?"

"Ah, but for you—"

So when people comment on it, on *them*, the assumption is "boyfriend," which she's always hasty to correct. But the only word she can find for the correction is "lover," with a sort-of smile, trying to express in a word just what she's trying to figure out now. Trouble is, this word has rather unfortunate romantic connotations. There's something very—Elizabethan about it, all wooing and sighing, "odes to his mistress' eyebrow," &c. *She*, however, means it in her own, very modern sense: sex, yes; friendship, after a fashion; but definitely no love. Bit of a misnomer, huh?

She remembers once asking him about it. He was actually the one to prompt it, unconsciously—

"Yeah, I used to go there with one of my other girlfriends," he said, casually—she's forgotten what they were talking about, because *that*—that made her freeze.

"Was that you suggesting I'm now your girlfriend?" is what she doesn't say; instead, "Hey . . . what do you call 'us'? I mean, like, *this*, you and me, what we're doing."

He doesn't really seem to get it. "*We're* not anything, we just—*are*. This, us, hasn't—it's not yet anything that needs a name."

"But what do you say to other people?"

"I don't talk about you to other people."

Impossible man! Why can't he see that what she wants to know is what *she's* supposed to call it?

"Don't get me wrong, sweetheart," she wishes she'd said, later, once she's had time to think about it, to think about *why* she wants—needs?—to define him, them, whatever it is they're doing. "I wasn't hoping you'd ask me to be your *girl*friend or anything—I don't want a 'relationship,' with anyone, and certainly not with you. But it would be nice to have a word for—whatever this is, to answer those awkward questions. Not for us, not for me—hell, call me your whore if you like, makes no difference to me—but just to have *something* to tell other people. I'm not bothered about people in general—I actually rather enjoy the weird looks I get when I'm with you. But, people I know, especially people *we* know, having something to say other than 'not-boyfriend' would definitely make it easier."

She tries again: another evening, another bottle of vodka, or most thereof, having been consumed. "You know how I asked what you call us?"

She's sitting on the bed, addressing his back while he fiddles with the music, barely paying attention to her. She doesn't like that.

"Well, you see, someone called you my boyfriend. I wanted to correct him—I said, you're not my boyfriend—but I didn't have anything with which to correct him."

He stood up while she was explaining. He's looking at her now, trying to see where she's going with this.

"I guess . . . I'm not sure there is a word for you, for what we are or what we have." Gaining confidence. "Maybe we should make one up." She laughs. "Let us . . . *neologize* together." (A friend had once praised her ability to make any word she chooses sound utterly filthy, an ability of which she makes great use.)

He smiles, at last, and comes over to her. She recognizes that smile. He crouches in front of her, his hands on her knees.

"Oh, I'll neologize you, baby," he says, pushing her legs apart.

Later, she will wonder. Is he deliberately avoiding the subject because he finds it difficult, awkward? Or does it genuinely not interest him? His expressions are, for the most part, impossible to decipher. She can never tell what he's thinking— except when he wants her to. It's almost as if, by being so open about so much of himself, he's trying to satisfy her curiosity—if he gives her enough of him, she won't ask for, she won't *take* any more.

"So what are you hiding from me, my dear?" she asks him when he's not there. "What are you so desperate for me not to see?"

ANTONIA KLIMENKO

Reproduction

It was
as if
he had gone to sleep
for the last time
inside the painting, itself,
as if
he had pulled up
the misshapen hills for blankets,
blankets dripping with green muddied sorrow,
as if
he had succumbed
to the pull of Earth's opaque forces,
painted himself under irresistible layers
of cerulean blue
and laid himself
down in it.

Out of the swirling darkness—a shock of light:
golden, glorious, illuminating, sweeping—
a ladder reaching up and
out of
the sagging, caving roof of his madness,
reaching beyond
the deaf ear
of its simple wooden frame.
Yes, that topped it off.

Antonia Klimenko

I read somewhere that thieves
used a ladder to reach the roof
of the Van Gogh Museum. Perhaps,
they wished to climb into one of his paintings.

"What's the name of that one?" you asked.
"Hilltop," I replied.
Surrender to the Earth, I thought.
It was
as if
it was.

SAM LANGER

Poem

"It's not much but it's all we've got," she said & passed me
a snapped tin comb
I found the inscription *he did not return*
until six in the evening, the result had to be personal
in the only sense of the word
tweaking us to the mountains outside, changing us
as it were into beasts.
He accepted everything
people brought him
equally troubled by the bright lights
and half a bottle of eau-de-vie
on her dark table

It finds me "he thought of himself as a table
a parade of dishes stood on slopes
of the mountain."
His aunt as forward and sour as his dry walk
charring slowly in the fire, we would treat
the rich foreign merchants differently, musty . . .
I start each day with turns
and turns for a few seconds
sinking like the invention of a dog on the slopes
the swamps dragged him sobbing the plain from,
shielding his red eyes with one arm, his final entity
in the eye. To feel a keen concern, to listen
to some light romantic Symphony—
but where was she? He asked the Rose

but it played dumb, grudging him
even petty silence. It was going.
Maybe there was no salvation in this world, only
the fall of it toward the loins. And I drew
akin to Sam in this respect,
at least. She looked up from the curve
of a gradually descending figure, the smooth sauces
and span surfaces of her kitchen reminded him quietly
complained quietly of the early hour
the sun outside was jets
the garden twitched through glass
she circled the sunny corner for a sick winter guest
he ran fingers through crisp hair
his eyes narrowed thoughtfully on her face.

Illustrated Feet

and the therefore voices in court
brackets cold into showoff the drills
elephant the pedestal
refer to dyes party
a pond stung under informal branches of the white tree

martin pill find evening no problem
between will and sweating there an agreement
seeps confusion trumps
your old flagstone home
poured you out a priest in the jeans of man

but you got around to her face
rarely pointing out the ground composer
no need was portraits no rum mate announcements
a father bed extinguished in the famous belt

a body sets
awe it is schism of eye
porch over it helps
numb the epochs
glazed abdomen
tanned ice

JUDITH CHRIQUI

Holiday

Tel Aviv, Israel

You weren't there the following morning, the morning I awoke feeling strange. At first, I thought this strangeness may have been warranted; I had done things the night before I shouldn't have. I did those things because I wanted to fall asleep with ease. I didn't want to be the last one awake in my city. I wanted to look the way my roommate looked when she slept. Peaceful, one long yellow curl cradling her face like a half moon. That night, I watched her with red eyes. I watched her until I'd forgotten I'd been watching her, until I slept.

I awoke in pain. My head pounded with unbearable resonance, my face felt drained and white, as though throughout the night I had been sweating colour. My room was like a box, one of many. I imagined another box stacked on top of mine, and one on each side, and so forth. The building had once served as an absorption center for poor immigrants; now it was my home, and would remain my home for the rest of the year.

I had to recover quickly. Soon my aunt would be waiting downstairs. I would go with her; I would be staying with her for the holiday. I had to recover quickly.

I phoned a friend, who I knew would be awake. I told her I needed to eat something. We walked to the shopping mall down the street; another friend came. I said, Crazy night. And I told them where I had been, what I had done, but not everything. I excluded the part about the thing I had done that I shouldn't have. I ate silently. They spoke—of what I can't remember. They said, Let's go. So we left. I was trying to grasp how I felt but couldn't. I kept walking. Slowly nausea turned into lightheadedness and then dizziness. The girls had gained speed, or I had slowed down. There was a bench ahead of me. It must have known that I would need it. It must have known what was coming.

That feeling came. That feeling that I would come to know so deeply, that feeling that I am now betrothed to, that doom, that wave. It was a wave. I sat down. My heart was suddenly too alive, and I had this tingling sensation throughout my body. As though the very hand of God were reaching inside my chest, squeezing thunder from my heart.

What's wrong? The girls asked. Why are you sitting there? I said, I don't know, I feel dizzy. They said, Put your head between your legs. I did, and then I felt like I was falling, that if I closed my eyes I would die. And my parents, I loved them. I thought, How shameful it is to die like this. One of the girls spoke, I'll bring you water. I noticed she was afraid, and that in turn made me more afraid. Then, suddenly, another wave of dizziness passed through me. My heart raged inside my chest. I said, I have to tell you something. I did something last night. It isn't really anything, and I didn't even want to do it, but I did and now my heart will burst. I think I'm dying.

I kept having to re-position myself on the bench, so I wouldn't die. I was sure if I closed my eyes . . . My friend shuffled back with the water. I drank the whole bottle; everything. Nothing changed. A man passed by. He said, Are you okay? I said, No. He said, Shall I call you an ambulance? I said, Yes, call me an ambulance. I began to cry. Though I may have already been crying.

My aunt arrived at the hospital three hours later. She said, Are you okay. I said, Yes, I am okay. I'm sorry. I cried again. The blood tests came back negative; there was nothing wrong with me. I didn't think to ask, What was it then? What happened to me? I left with my aunt. She said, Are you going to tell your mother? I said, No she will worry. My aunt said, Okay, it's your decision. She told my mother.

Antalya, Turkey

A girl told me a story. She was staying at her grandfather's apartment after he had passed away. She was nearly asleep when she heard the sound of running water.

She went out to look and saw that the sink had been turned on. She turned it off and went back to sleep . . . until the sound returned again. She said she knew who it was: it was he. Your Grandfather? I asked. Yes, she said, It was he. You weren't scared? I said. No, she said. And that terrified me most.

Now there I was lying in bed. I was in the hotel with you. You rose from bed, went to the bathroom and closed the door. Suddenly the bedroom went completely dark. And that's when I felt that wave again. It had returned.

I tried lying in bed. But my heart gained speed inside my chest. I felt God again; I felt His cold hand. And then I worried that the sink in the room would turn on. I said to myself, If the sink turns on, then I don't know what I will do. I will be so afraid. I will go crazy. I will lose myself. The room went silent. You came back to the bed. You didn't know how afraid I was. I kept it from you, because I didn't want you to know. I didn't want to remind you of those drugs, and how you hate them, and how you hate that I did them that night. I tried to turn on the television. You said, No, sleep. I said, I can't. You didn't respond. Then I thought about the sink again. I kept thinking about the sink. If it turns on . . . it's going to turn on, a ghost is going to turn it on, there is a ghost here. It's going to turn on. I have to get up and watch it and make sure no one turns it on. If it does, then what? I will lose myself, I will go crazy. I placed my hands tightly over my ears.

I went into the closet and turned on the light. I sat on the floor and read. I was reading. I read. I couldn't read; my heart was racing. My heart was going. I called out to you. I woke you. I said, I don't know what's wrong. I am scared. You said, Come here, and you tried to hold me. But I wanted to move and I couldn't stay there. I said, No. I got up. You said, What's wrong. I said, I don't know. I'm scared. My heart is racing. You said, Why? I said, I don't know. You said, Well, don't jump off the balcony. I became angry. You didn't understand. I said, I need to walk. So I left the room and walked around the hotel. I went to the bar. I thought, Alcohol will slow my heart down. But no, the opposite. I felt worse. As I was walking back I felt dizzier. Don't close your eyes, I thought. Stay awake. Stay awake. I returned to the room, you said, Come sleep now. I said, I can't. You heard a pill bottle rattling. My mother had given me some medication for the plane ride, because I was afraid of flying and it made me calm. I resolved then to take a half of a pill. You said, What are you doing? I said, You're right, I don't know. I thought I would take this because I don't know what's happening to me and—

Don't take that, you said. You are fine. I said, You are right, but I'm sorry. I took half. You went to sleep. I lay in bed awake, holding your hand, watching the clock. I fell asleep at eight a.m. I woke up at ten. I was fine. Everything was fine.

Tel Aviv, Israel

It returned. We had been watching a movie and, in the movie, one of the characters, a girl, goes crazy. She cuts herself; she cuts her body, and goes to the church to expose herself. When she opened her robe, we stopped the video. You said, What's wrong. I said, That feeling again. I had to stand to up. I couldn't sit down because I was afraid of becoming too relaxed, of letting the feeling win. I was sure I would die. Something is trying to kill me, I thought. Shall I call an ambulance? I wondered. Or my resident advisor? But we are on a holiday. She won't be here. I took two pills in secret. You said, Let's eat something. I said, Okay. We went. And then you told me that I should bless the food. I said, Why? You said, Because it will taste better. It tasted better. I couldn't believe it. It was only chicken. Chicken tastes better blessed, I cried. I wept. It tastes better, I said. I am okay now.

I awoke the next morning afraid. I was so terrified of the feeling returning that I made it return. I said, I can't move now. I can't leave the house. You said, It's Sukkoth. Come to the Sukkah. Talk to the Rabbi. On the walk there we passed the mall and I felt paralyzed again. I said, I'm having trouble walking, I can't walk. You said, Almost there. I said, But I can't. I took another pill. We arrived. I cried to you. I told you, I need to go to the doctor now.

Philadelphia, Pennsylvania

My father knew that I had been sick, but he was in denial of its extremity, and unaware of how it had really begun (we chose to conceal it from him, my mother and I). I wept to my father, and berated him for not detecting the blatant signs of my childhood anxiety. For watching in silence as it built up, and then tumbled down without warning. My father said, I raised you well. You cannot blame me for this. You have done this to yourself. And then he said, I don't understand. Your home is your kingdom. You should feel safe here. I said, But I don't. I'm afraid here. I've been afraid for a long time. I slept upstairs for years, because I was too afraid to sleep in my own room. You didn't think there was anything strange about that? I didn't notice, he said. You didn't want to notice, I said. And now this. But you are on medication now, he said; you shouldn't be having any more attacks. Why can't you help me? I asked. He said, I don't know. I said, Get out. And he left.

Rio de Janeiro, Brazil

It was the summer after my year in Israel. I came here to see you for the last time. The night I arrived, I cried to you deeply without reason, and then again, alone. Your sister ate cherries and spoke to me of your dead mother while you were in the shower. You never spoke of your mother, and I had always thought this was strange. Every time I asked about her, you would say, No, I am not ready yet. But are you not yet twenty-five? I would ask. No, you would answer, I am not twenty-five, and anyway, it doesn't matter.

You didn't drive so we took the bus everywhere. At the end of my trip, I would come to understand that this was the single activity in which I took most pleasure. Once, on a bus on the way to Barra, I looked out the window and cried gazing at the coastline. Small mountains fastened like giant almonds in the sea. The water was flat, and glistened in perfect silence.

JEFFREY GREENE

Cooking Octopus with Madame Esteves

After years of thinking our building distinctly hostile, I notice that the young blonde, fourth floor in building C, perpendicular to building B, mine, is topless, shaking a bathroom mat out an open window. We seem to assent to new neighbourly roles, exhibitionist and voyeur respectively, but for all I know there are gawking neighbours above and below me. Madame Esteves, our Portuguese *femme de ménage*, is vacuuming violently enough to send my small cat and Maltese dog scrambling for refuge in my study, knocking over stacked books and papers. I know Madame Esteves would like to change my habits, to invade my unkempt personal domain and scold me about scattering clothing, but ultimately she respects the cramped space I occupy in peaceful chaos. She manages to keep the other two rooms decent enough, and she washes my badly worn tennis shoes, sews the crotch back into my jeans, and balls my socks as if I were a child.

Madame Esteves vacuums her way to the threshold of my study and looks critically out the window at a majestic chestnut tree in our courtyard that towers far above the sixth-floor roofs. Victor Hugo once painted the tree, a *tableau* that now hangs in his namesake museum in the Marais. I regard it as a private tree of life, tuned to the seasons and filled with ring-necked doves, city pigeons, and raucous magpies, the latter prompting irate residents to hurl various objects through the branches at them. Madame Esteves declares, "Do you realize how dangerous that tree is? Imagine a storm at night. Imagine it falling directly into your apartment when you are sleeping." What I do realize is that she and I see two different planes of reality: she sees a malevolent tree, and I see the undressed body of my neighbour who has retreated but continues a shadowy parade across three windows.

Madame Esteves comes every Wednesday and Friday. The dog and cat with uncanny hearing herald Madame Esteves's arrival as she taps the code and clicks the door open to a hall paved with stone between a dress store called Future Maman, fashion for pregnant women, and a Paris branch of a mysterious international investment agency that requires merely a Spartan desk, phone, and PC for its business.

She takes the coffin-sized, wagon-green elevator; rings the doorbell; and simultaneously unlocks the door calling out, *Bonjour monsieur!* Just by the tone of her voice, those words, *Bonjour monsieur,* her greeting me before I make it out of my study to grab my deranged white dog, I sense whether she's had another family catastrophe. Whenever I hear the slow descending notes, almost moaned, *Bon—jour—mon—sieur,* I know that the barometric level of her soul has bottomed out with the arrival of some new emotional ordeal.

Madame Esteves is a small woman in her late fifties, with dark Iberian features, not at all unattractive. While she works as a guardian for her own building in the fifth *arrondissement,* she also cleans for four families and is in great demand. As a rule she does not clean for residents in her building, fearing that she would be at their beck and call for every imaginable service. She has lived in France for over twenty years, coming with her husband, a mason.

Every Wednesday we spend some time talking in our adopted language, both of us permanent residents in a foreign land. She speaks freely about her family and her life back in the hills just below Coimbra in northern Portugal, in a village called Miranda do Corvo. I like to listen and practise my French since my lessons ended abruptly. I'd had a private teacher who lived on the eleventh floor of a modern building near Plaisance. One recent session, I arrived at her apartment, and she'd barricaded the windows with her furniture. She led me to her small cell-like bed, suddenly *tutoyer*ing me, forcing me to adjust my verbs while I was being undressed and my hands pressed to her undernourished ass. Middle-aged, balding, teeth so badly capped that no one understands me, French or English, I'm not the type women chase unless they happen to become unhinged, a phenomenon more difficult to decipher in a foreign language though the barricaded windows should have been a dead giveaway.

When Madame Esteves feels upbeat, she talks about almost anything, from tutelary advice about homeopathic medicines for colds to her father in his nineties, still working the vineyards in Portugal by hand. However, even when she is in a good mood, the conversation often turns mildly morose. "Yes, the pills work, but each spring I catch the flu anyway." Or "It's sad that young people have no interest in working the land like my papa. It bores them. They go off to Lisbon. What can they know of the earth without touching it? Everything suffers. No wonder the vegetables have no flavour. No one wants to touch the earth anymore."

Sometimes she talks about the artists and writers she has known in Paris. She wants to make it clear to me that she is cultured. "You know who Pessoa is? *Le grand poète portugais*. He lived in Lisbon, and now his house is a museum." So we talk about Pessoa, who was so fond of Whitman and who explored identity throughout his career in three totally different personas.

Madame Esteves returns to her list of sculptors and architects for whom she cleaned when the elevator alarm rings. I know just by the panicky persistence that it's Madame Dubois, fifth floor, eighties, in sheer hysterics. Our capricious elevator seems to be on a mission to entomb the poor old woman between the third and fourth floors forcing me to coo reassurances that the elevator expert will liberate her, if and when he arrives. Madame Esteves stands behind me, arm on my shoulder offering encouragement.

At around six p.m., I usually leave the apartment to shop at our local *commerçants* or at the Grande Epicerie, one of the best-known food markets in Paris. While I unpack the groceries on returning, Madame Esteves scolds, "No, no, don't market at the Bon Marché! Everything is too expensive. You come home with almost nothing for fifty Euros."

"But everything is so sumptuously displayed. Besides, it gets me out of the apartment," I offer defensively, knowing she is absolutely right.

"So, what are you making?"

When I say "*du poisson*," Madame Esteves stops her ironing to describe Portuguese recipes for mackerel, sardines, and trout, all of which are by far the most affordable fish. She is particularly proud of her cooking and informs me of the soups and various dishes she prepares for some of the older people in her building. She offers to cook for me, seeing that I was on the threshold of destroying a perfectly good piece of overpriced fish.

I manage to resist Madame Esteves's offer to prepare my dinner. Nevertheless, I ask her if she knows a good recipe for octopus. I love octopus in tapas or salads, but when I market I am reluctant to buy one of the large grayish pools of flaccid tentacles. Even the fishmonger, holding up the mass like a sad mop and calling it a *belle bête*, a beautiful beast, doesn't help me to overcome my trepidation. Besides, I have always sympathized with octopuses since they blush and have oddly knowing eyes. Madame Esteves assures me that she knows the secret to cooking octopus and is eager to bring an octopus and give me a Portuguese cooking lesson.

As soon as Madame Esteves leaves, I open a bottle of Pouilly-Fume and drink most of it while gazing at the evening sun catching the limbs of the tree that might crash into my apartment. In the midst of my musings, my neighbour Nadia has an inconvenient emergency. Of course, all emergencies are inconvenient, particularly when I'm drunk. Her beautiful Norwegian forest cat has kidney failure, refuses to eat, and therefore must be driven to the vet. Nadia is one of those confusing French clichés that populate my neighbourhood, a voluptuous French woman, nearly seventy, who can compete with women thirty years her junior for turning heads. She calls only when she needs something, which adds something to her mystique. She insists that she needs me and not the cab I suggest. Besides, we share a weakness for animals. In the pale green waiting room of the clinic, Nadia's body gives off the moist radiance of grief.

Nadia had been a nature documentary producer for the France 2 television chain. I tried to distract her from her dying cat by discussing octopuses. I said, "I once saw a television program that showed Greek fishermen catching octopuses by tying ropes to terracotta pots and dropping them into the Aegean. Did you know that they can't resist snug spaces? The pot that they make into a seemingly secure home turns out to be a trap." She pretends not to understand my French, puts her head on my shoulder.

On Wednesday, when Madame Esteves comes, she hardly notices the animals greeting her and moans despondently, *Bon—jour, mon—sieur*. She is completely pale as if she hasn't slept since I had seen her the week before. The gravity of her planet seems to have doubled. As soon as I ask, "Are you all right?" she bursts into tears. This week she was supposed to bring an octopus and teach me how to cook it as she would in Portugal.

"My husband is depressed. He is agitated all night. When he sleeps, he has nightmares. I can't be in the same room with his nightmares. Things are better during the day. But he's tired and unhappy. He doesn't eat what I make for him. He doesn't care for it. He wants to go back to Portugal, to his family in the country. But our children are here in Paris. What can one do? Life is never easy, is it? *C'est dur.*"

"There may be medicine for this," I offer.

"The doctors give him tests, a brain scan, some medicines. Only time seems to work. Then he's better for a while."

"What does he do when he's well?" I ask.

"He looks at paintings all day. For three years before he retired, he repaired stonework on the Louvre. While he was working, he fell in love with the paintings he saw inside through the windows." The retired Portuguese mason, chronically depressed, spends his time haunting canvases in the galleries and museums of Paris.

On Fridays, Madame Esteves works for only two hours. I always leave out postage stamps for her: tigers, birds, airplanes, and landscapes. She had seen that I was throwing out envelopes that came from foreign countries, and she explained that her granddaughter was collecting stamps. "She wants to be a travel agent."

Madame Esteves arrives on a Friday, pale and stricken. "My son was hospitalized. He was beaten. Bones in his face, around the eye, were broken. Who knows what's next? Each day I wake up and it's a war."

"How did it happen?"

The tears begin. "It happened at a stoplight at Bastille. It was a traffic argument, and two men took my son out of the car and beat him. He lies on the couch and is afraid to leave the apartment."

"Paris has changed."

"Who knows what's next?"

Her son's beating at Bastille seems excessive for mere road rage, particularly by French standards. I wonder about drugs. Madame Esteves repeats "No luck" followed by "This world isn't put together right." I hold her until she relaxes, but on returning to my study I can hear her sob.

The telephone rings. It's my French teacher's mother. I learn that I was the last to see her daughter before the police had to breech the barricaded door and coax her to the hospital. In fact, I was the only person to see her for weeks. My French teacher's mother wants to meet at a café to talk. Agreeing, I note time and address, catching out of the corner of my eye my naked neighbour.

My Friday routine includes making the rounds to three *poissonneries*, the fish vendors in our neighbourhood, along with the four stands on the various market days on the Boulevard Raspail. Le Dome is perhaps the most extraordinary and the most expensive *poissonnerie* in Paris, with the fish arranged in beautiful shining patterns and sprayed periodically as if the counters formed an exotic garden.

Oddly none of the three neighbourhood *poissonneries* sell octopus, whereas most of the fish stands at the Raspail open markets carry it. I asked the fishmonger to help me choose a *belle bête*. It's hard to gauge the size of an octopus since they are displayed upside down in a star-like bed of arms. The one I buy looks huge when the fishmonger, grinning, assuring me that nothing could be more beautiful, finally held it up. He pours the animal into a plastic sack, throws in some lemons, and wishes me *Bon weekend!* as I carry off the hefty animal back to the apartment.

The octopus broods in the sink until Madame Esteves arrives. "*Quelle belle bête!*" Madame Esteves is nearly ecstatic. She removes the beak and ink sacks and cleans the suckers that even in death manage to cling to your skin. I think of how she said, "No one wants to touch the earth. That is why everything has lost its flavour." How sensual that seems: touch and flavour. Madame Esteves prepares a *court bouillon* with a carrot, bay leaf, half an onion, garlic, parsley, and peppercorns. She explains, "Never add salt. It detaches the skin."

Madame Esteves lifts the octopus out of the sink, the tentacles drooping more than a half-meter long. "You have to dunk the octopus several times to help make it tender." She holds the beast over the large stockpot and begins plunging it into the boiling *court bouillon*. The tentacles instantly come to life, turning dark, purplish, and coiling, some form of contraction in the dead cells. All the while Madame Esteves, almost in tears, shrieks out, "Look, I'm a witch! I'm a witch!"

COLIN MAHAR

When I Have the Wind In My Skull
translation of Boris Vian

When I have the wind in my skull
When I have the wind on my bones
Perhaps then, I'll believe in the dull
Editions of my future tomes.
How I will miss it
My elemental plastic
Plastic tic tic
and my face devoured by rats.
This pair of lips
eyebrows, eyelids
my thighs and the ass upon which I sit.
My hair, my fists,
my pretty blue eyes
my hooded eyes.
So I bequeath to you
my roman nose
my heart, my liver, my spleen
all my admirable nothings
for which I was so admired
by Dukes and Duchesses
By Popes and Popesses
Abbotts and Abbesses
and tradespeople.
And more, I'll no longer be
this moist, radiant
brain, which served me,

which imagined me dead;
the green bones, the windswept skull,
Ah, how I hate to grow old.

Emily Dickinson Re-translations
d'après *Claire Malroux*

I.

That Love is all there is
is all we know of Love
and that's enough, it's mark is made
and to its measure paid.

II.

This morning comes just Once
But imagines coming twice
Two Dawns for a Single Morning;
Giving Life a Sudden Price

III.

To Marry one's self to Virtue
Is a Discrete and Pleasant Union
But Nature relishes her Roses
As she continues to Consume them.

IV.

Of Glory not a thing survives
Though Eternal are its scars—
The Asterix is for the Dead
The Living have the Stars

V.
Is it too late, my Dear, to touch you?
Here's a moment we once knew—
Oceanic Love, Terrestrial Love,
and the Love of Heaven too.

Nocturne

I'm thinking of
the heat in the reins
a gear in love with itself
two parts that fit
I'm thinking about your face:
there's nothing to invent
Driven to distraction
or just walking there
The edge of my mind
against the edge of yours
An astrolabe isn't thinking
of a concrete lane
or unconquerable interior
Abiding by its class
and country church, a kitsch picture
is not "sincerity"
though I am native to it
A nation has this sound
of being born   The human
is not its ill-begotten ad
A hemisphere is not your hair
in its Parisian rooms
An astrolabe is not
a metaphor for love
though love contain the mortal roots
of congress, like a peasant
inside the name you give its ruins

Another Life in Green

Outbreaks of calumny
have not yet killed the lupine
Trying to make up
for a sudden lack of air
the hill grows thin
against its grid
closing its eyes
painting its gardens
Man and not-man
hardly correspond at all
When a character says
"I am not Romantic"
it's because an imaginary
line has crossed his heart
The willed adventure
of the alpine grass
The distant lightning
of a *coup d'état*

Elizabeth Willis

The Skirt of Night

A painted tree shadows the river. In a compound eye,
nature leans away from struggle, the name is implied. See
how he is taken by one hand, or by his leg, a starry gas
beating overhead. From the eastern balcony, horizon blinks
like a bug. The paradox of counting spreads its ink across
the page, a signature more built than drafted. To see or not
see. Do you read or hear it? As if by hunger, earth empties
its mind.

MEGAN FERNANDES

Constellations

"Meet me by the sand dune
and bring the yellow umbrella,"

you stole to me before the heavy
weight of sleep. But I did not.

I prefer transporting in small kitchens,
baked in oven heat,

and the scuttle of dishes shifting.
I wait there, for I know the chances

of you at the sand dune
are slim. Even the smallest whim

or whiff of apricot scones
may reroute your soggy travels.

I search all of Venice Beach.
I duck the fold, the bite,

the catastrophe of gestures.
I peek above the carousels

which wound the bodies into
a triangular blur, but I could

not make out the
smell of your lines.

I spot the giantess
in the lime polka dot dress,

and ask her if she has seen you.
But perched high upon the California

elephant rock,
my wail is smothered in her

petticoat dreams,
and with one quiet leap

she flies past me-
pulling, tugging, freeing,

a gigantic tumbling sheet
of moody stars

across the sky.
And it is dark.

So to Rue Buffon I stumble,
where stands three walls

and all of them will outlive me.
The museum of the outliving

in the basement edge of the city
on a flat untextured map.

The fourth wall, in the puddled alley,
the backstage, I lean.

where jurassic players have their fortunes read,
where the panes are dusty and teal

with neglect.
I press code in the murky concrete,

trace the "tug and displace"
of matter, until I hear it.

And the sounds grows.
I hear not yellow,

but the soft blue of your organ speech,
which lifts me.

"We ate pomegranate seeds
and wet guacamole"

you whisper
in warm stillness.

I check for sand in your mane,
eager to discover your detours.

Ella

When I see you
perhaps I should mention
that I have been
dreaming of your furniture,
more specifically your
baby blue carpets,
hardwood floors,
mirrors and porcelain,
all of them sick in green fog.
I dream often that you
are in bed with your father,
your eyes bulging
with cartoon leaks,
your mother in her
white nightgown,
crying to the soft tile
in the wind
of your childhood bathroom.

Perhaps I should mention
that I am dreaming of your
baby grand brown piano
and the enormous Russian
who would press our fingers
to anonymous keys
in meaningless webbed sounds
so pain and flesh collapsed

into notes and later,
with improvement,
an arpeggio.

What was the melody we
could never assemble?
What was the melody we
could never live without?
A Venetian Boat Song—
wrung out
of our trembling hands.

We came to hate Russia
and associated it with
ivory graves,
steep in ached sound
and
heaviness
in our fingertips.

Red Umbrellas at *La Nuit Blanche*

An outdoor installation by Noel Dolla at the Parc des Buttes Chaumont,
Paris, France, October, 2010.

Seven hundred red umbrellas in a graceful lean,
reclining in rows across the northern hill of the park,
sticking their blush tongues out to the night stars,
expecting what? On their sides, coquettish, as if lids

half winking, as if legs half spread, a tango skirt lifted,
their spiked frames edging up against their neighbours
in this repeat of red. Or perhaps ruby mushroom heads
sprouting in graveyard formation, crimson tombstones.

Like a tilted cabaret show in this flirtatious moonlit row,
they blow clumsy kisses, inch slightly, swaying to one side,
this tease of movement from objects so enjoying their
own spectacle. They actually look happy. And how seldom

do they get to lean and seep and yawn, deep into manicured
grass, getting their metal arms muddy? The umbrellas laze,
breathy and indifferent from their usual call to action—
for how often do their faceless blooms gaze into a clear sky?

(Kinetics) of the pink leaf

To measure the cellular breath
of a pink leaf
one must imagine the
little tunnels of xylem and phloem
which look like asparagus subways
transporting weary hydrogen
and oxygen atoms
decked in fedora hats.
Or some femme fatale nutrient
off to reap a lover in soil,
her mitochondria shaking
in the root pressure.

Microtubules are important
for their surface area
and act as
little trampolines for quantum leaps.
They are hypothesized to be
the smallest unit of sensation,
their coral tails assembled in cylinders
to uphold the integrity of the cytoskeleton
and to perform the position of Moses
for the other organelles.

Tucked in the cellular membrane,
are dreamy oval purple proteins
from my biology book,
structures that looked like
picky eggplants with bruised soft spots
for sodium and potassium channels.

How delicious to study the tissue of what is,
to make maps and labyrinths and high school
rivalries between molecules,
I always thought benzenes
were disguised ferris wheels and
secretly craved
the carnival of formlessness.

SARAH RIGGS

From "Letters to the Dead"

Dear Virginia,

I thought of you as I was getting out of the bath, not of a novel but of the years, how they fill or flatten, the happier we are the faster time goes. I thought of horizontality, the precision of illness, your need for space universalized to Kantian proportions, your fear of wards, of repetition, of the repetition of wars, nearby, of the poetry journal you nearly had, the children you wished to have—what would they have been like? and I think of the men, the servants, the lighthouse, the strength of Mrs. Dalloway and Ramsay, in all that flux, that hyperspeed of emotions, held by the stature, the static, the love, of a man, a husband, a degree of verticality in all that horizontality, that knowledge of the ill, the dying, the morose, the melancholic, the alcoholic, that intimate knowledge of the sky, the waves, water, waves.

I am glad you left a note for Leonard. I have found it many times in my mind, and I want you back. I don't know you at all. But I have plagiarized you till you've become me. The day I finished *To the Lighthouse* the fifth summer in a row, along a path of diminishing novel reading, we started to look for an actual lighthouse. To visit. To fill. To try. Goodbye, Virginia. Those I have loved extremely well become part of me. And I have learned to feel what it is to swim.

From "Letters to the Dead"

Dear Demeter,

For years I invited you for visits, it was not your fault. You looked in the drawers at the forks, it was the excitement. I came out of you and into the world but we grew up in a house of staircases, it only made sense that I would climb, both up and down.

The rendered panes cannot be further broken or displaced. We are down here and it is dark. It is the way of the world to be under itself even as it overdoes it.

We can't be together. I can't be saved. Nor you.

But there is spring: the hyacinth, the forsythia, the pansy, outside of 139 Pelleport. The spring is on its way in the form of a rabbit we saw in the metro entry at Bastille, eating lettuce on cardboard.

Sea Quince

Here are tidepools, some slate rock, a small
dead crab. The soft stones are red yellowish grey.
There's a rust orange unnameable
(hawkweed), oxeye, daisies, buttercup, white
iris, chives, meadow grass. "An ocean
of seaweed," snails spotted the size of
wide grains of sand, rockweed flung and spread,
waterbirds, barnacles on the rusted spheres
of the loading dock supports, some rock slime
walking on multiple small rocks to stay
the slippage, pigeons scattering from underneath, a cinematic impression
of being under what's submerged at times,
being called back (knowing I would be)

but by the mother's call: solitude at ease with attachment

JULIE KLEINMAN

Young Woman in Window, Reflected

A preparation. She sits alone, her back not quite against the chair, stiffened. Books, hardwood floors, two low armchairs facing each other—it is familiar by now, enough so that her gaze is not as piqued, her alertness almost sags. No table to put her wine glass on, so she places it gingerly on the floor, and as she hears his footsteps return she floods her gaze across to the shelves, as if thinking unaware about something she sees. He sighs and sits down, and after a few silent moments, she looks up at him as if caught deep in thought, surprised by his sudden presence. She smiles. He sips his wine. He says—

Something, but she misses it, concentrating on leaning forward and listening. Inhaling, he continues, as if to answer her furrowed brow, she knows she need not speak, for he will continue with his own ideas whether or not she responds to them.

It's not always like this. She wants to listen, really listen, but there are so many things to think about. He looks at her, scrutinizing. Smiling again, sipping her wine, she shakes her head and looks down at the floor.

"More wine?" he asks. Before she murmurs yes, he is standing up, reaching across the space between them, briefly brushing her elbow as he reaches for her glass. While his face is turned pouring, she closes her eyes, breathing, trying to understand what she could be doing here, in her professor's house. He pats her on the head indulgently before giving her glass back, asking, "Are you okay?" and smiling to himself.

"Just, you know, tired," she says, sipping the wine. He tells her stories of his college days, alluding to beautiful women who kept him from his work. She shudders, and looks at herself in the window behind his chair.

There are moments that repeat themselves when they talk. "You know," he'll begin, "I really feel that—" and here he'll pause, thinking. At these moments, she always tenses and holds her glass mid-sip, terrified of what might come next, that he is finally going to articulate—what?—and her cheeks will go red, and she won't know how to respond. The mid-breath silence drags on, her toes curled and suspended above the floor, purply wine ready to splash across the hardwood, waiting. Until he continues the thought and she settles into the chair and holds the wine between her knees, as if a terrible incident has just been avoided, and he continues unaware.

The train begins with a small shudder backwards before lurching into its smooth motion away from the yard, into the grey day. She pushes the curtain back to look out at the diminishing city, cloaked in rain and fog, the view partly obscured by her own blurry reflection. Behind her, a man talks loudly into his cellphone: "No, darling, the train should be on time and I'll take a cab to the apartment. I love you, too."

The conductor collects tickets, smiling and official. He looks down at her stack of books and papers in the seat next to her and shakes his head, saying, "Student, are you?" She nods automatically, and then shakes her head, smiles weakly. He moves on and she sees how purposefully he walks through the car.

Pressing her face against the window, she watches the crumbling city outskirts fall away into hills dotted with lifeless trees straggling out against the sky.

The wine swirls up and down in the glass, catching the outdoor lights in its wavering. You sit unopposed on the lawn, holding your glass at eye level. Around you, people sit in small groups on the grass, laughing and eating. "What legs this baby's got!" says a friend, shaking his glass. "Look at those legs," he exclaims, pointing to the red threads the wine leaves as it spins down. Everyone laughs, and John looks appreciatively toward his audience and says, in a low voice, something about a certain kind of red wine that has a particularly womanly aftertaste. You set your glass down and tilt your head curiously, wondering about the depth of those pungent whorls.

Someone makes a comment about you sitting there, looking at the wine like a lover. They speak in similes, constantly circling ideas. That talk about books you haven't read. You squeeze the backs of your arms and look hard at the wine, at the grass, at your food. "Really great soup," you tell Clara loudly. She smiles in lieu of thanks, and you take some more, awkward with the huge ladle.

John says: "Yes, Clara, and what is it I taste in here? Cumin, certainly, and perhaps a bit of dill and even nutmeg? And kale, great in this soup." Clara smiles again and they talk spices.

"It's really good, isn't it?" you say again, and they look at you, laughing and shaking their heads.

"Do you ever see that professor, that guy, anymore?" someone asks you. You say you haven't seen him since you graduated, no reason to talk now, no more classes. You try to sound casual but come off indignant. They gaze at you knowingly, and you stick your nose in the wine.

Posing, the other guests, in chairs and groups and circles. You wonder about friends, about posing. Rachel snorts on John's lap, freely tossing her head back into his arms. You have no lover to look at like wine, and you wonder what kind of womanly flavours you might exude, if any.

The train slows to the first station stop, the conductor walking briskly down the aisle, calling out the station name. She settles further into her seat as more passengers board, joining the murmur of the car. Although she is afraid that someone will sit with her, she cannot help but glance curiously at the parade of travellers as they move past her. A young woman pushes small children along in front of her while pulling a large suitcase; two teenage girls with backpacks talk in loud and excited gasps, standing on tiptoes to find two empty seats; two men in pinstripe suits, carrying briefcases, look back at her with equal curiosity.

The train moves out of the station as the passengers settle into their seats and she exhales, watching her breath cloud the window. She still has both seats for herself. The door at the end of the car slides open and a young man in a tweed jacket steps through and moves toward her. She directs her gaze to the window, hoping that he will pass by. His corduroy pants appear next to her reflection as he stops and asks if the seat is occupied. She looks up at him briefly, shaking her head no, obediently moving the books to the floor. He sits, looking toward her as if about to say something, but she looks quickly away, again out the window.

The hills get greener; the trees now have brightly coloured leaves. A red glimmer pushes behind the clouds into the day, and the occasional factories and train-line houses take on an autumnal tint as the sun moves toward the horizon.

She dances toward the stage, swinging her arms freely, remembering how much she loves live music. Laughing, clapping, swinging hips, falling into each other, and all under a common rhythm. A friend squeezes her shoulders and smiles, yelling to make herself heard, and the two girls dance together. The friend seems surprised to see her out here and says something, but the girl just laughs, for she cannot hear over the music.

"You know the drummer, don't you?" asks her friend.

"The drummer," she murmurs to herself. "Yes," she yells, "I knew him." They dance, unable to talk anymore, flailing and swinging. She feels the rhythm begin at the soles of her feet and push upward and outward, aching through her bones, released in movement.

The music stops, and she breathes out in quick gasps, exhausted. She looks to the stage, glancing up at the drummer as the crowd pushes her toward the exit. On her way out he blows her a kiss, and in a few moments he finds her outside, squeezing her shoulder hello. "Goodnight, *monsieur*," she says, tilting. And then, taking his hand she calls him *mon cheri,* graciously bowing, overdoing it. He hurt her long enough ago now that she can do that, murmur French salutations in his ear, falling out of reason, remembering when relationships made sense. He laughs, shaking his head, and she walks away smiling, heady with rhythm, into the coolness of early fall.

The train moves groggily, steadily through the countryside and sleepy small towns with their banks and post offices proudly columned and facing the tracks. She tries to avoid attempts at conversation from the young man, who tells her they have the same destination. He asks her about one of her books, he says that he's read it and didn't like it, what does she think? She lies and says she didn't like it much either, excusing herself to get some tea. Lights flicker on across the hills as the sky fills with purple twilight.

When she returns, he makes an elaborate gesture of getting out of the seat to let her in, taking her cup and handing it back to her after she sits down. She leans against the window, putting her tea on the foldout tray and curling into herself. He gets the message, it seems, and reads a news magazine.

She begins to fall asleep.

The young woman is sitting at her desk, reading, bent over and pushing the book into the mahogany. The words begin to blur, and she stretches her fingers across the pages, pressing harder, her eyes straining to follow the lines. As she flips the page a tear slips out and falls, disappearing into the binding. The moment it lands, she looks up sharply, startling herself.

Rising out of the chair, she walks to the bureau and begins to brush her hair in long, purposeful strokes. He told her once that she should put her hair in two braids, one on each side. "That looks cute," he said, "and so playful."

She parts her hair and carefully pulls half into an elastic, turning that side to the mirror and watching herself break the ponytail into three equal sections, crossing them over each other until she has run out of hair. She smoothes the braid down against her cheek and slowly performs the same task to the other side. In the mirror her eyes widen and their redness seems to lessen. The desk lamp casts a warm light over half of her face while the other half is overlain with shadow; very metaphoric, thinks the girl.

She takes out eyeshadow and brushes it across the dark eyelid, not able to tell what she's done. She adds eyeliner and more eyeshadow, very systematically, to both eyes, following with blush. Her friends have said she looks pale lately. Is she sick? they ask.

The blush is light pink-brown and called "nude nude"; she sweeps it down her cheekbones. As she opens the lipstick, she begins to wonder what she is doing, and her eyes gaze back inquisitively. She parts her lips and lets a moment pass before applying it in two quick strokes.

With unfaltering precision she places the compacts, then the brushes, back into a small black case. A mascara remains on her bureau; she is not sure if she should wear it tonight. She imagines herself dancing, sweat causing black rivulets of mascara to run down her cheeks. In the end, she puts it on anyway, swinging her braids playfully in the mirror and watching as she spreads a smile across her face, her eyes liquid with tears.

The train jerks into a mournful strain upward, rousing the girl from a dream. The young man next to her stirs suddenly as well, and she feels the muscles tighten up her spine. She sits rigid against the seat, one hand pressed into the book in her lap, her chin pointing straight at the seat in front of her, unmoving.

Looking out the passenger window while your mother is driving. Buildings open into parks with children playing. Soccer, slides, swings pushed by bubbly parents smiling down as they push higher and higher and higher. The man in the car next to you winks at you and you look sharply away, ashamed. Out of the corner of your eye you glance at your mother, driving, to make sure she has not witnessed the exchange.

She grips the wheel and looks ahead, set on the traffic and unsmiling. You glance again out the window; the man leers. Looking away, you begin to hunch forward, inching toward the dashboard.

"What in God's name are you doing," says your mother. You sit up again and bite back tears. Swallowing knots, you don't want her to know about the man. Eyes straight ahead then, at neither your mother nor the man. You try to remember to look only out in front of you, but that's hard and you keep forgetting.

The traffic is tight so the cars inch forward; your mother bangs her wrist on the steering wheel. Cars are cutting in and out amidst honks and yells; the city is swarming and wild at this hour. Your mother's friend Kathy, visiting from the country, tries to follow close behind you but she is not used to these streets. She starts honking and waving, and when you look at her in the rearview mirror she looks scared, like screaming for help.

Suddenly your mother is opening the door and running back toward Kathy's car. A moment passes and you freeze, when everything begins to collide. Man in the other car, traffic moving, car idling, no mom. The man begins to open his door. You scream.

Your mother returns to find you screaming, a low-pitch, steady wail. "How could you . . . ?" you blubber, "Why did you leave, what if . . . what were you . . . why—?" the words tumble with your tears toward your feet.

"Don't be so damn touchy," says your mother in a tense burst. You hunch your shoulders and inch your body into itself, wishing you could disappear.

The train is speeding along assuredly to its final destination. She has fallen asleep, but awakens to the young man nudging her shoulder, whispering. "We're almost there," he says. She stretches and blinks, displaced for a moment, unsure where "there" is. Her dreams from the shallow sleep echo vaguely in her mind; she knows she has been dreaming, but of what? Only blurry shapes and outlines remain. The darkness is so full now that she can see nothing outside, only herself, eyes clouded in the window. The train slows and the conductor announces the final station stop.

She lines up with the other passengers, knowing that soon they will rise up into the station to be met by a crowd of smiling faces. There will be welcoming hugs and bags will be carried for the weary travellers. The doors open and she walks toward the bright lights with assurance, secure in the knowledge that no one familiar will be there waiting, and that soon she will walk out into the night alone.

Waking to the rain, I float upstairs expecting good mornings, but the house is silent. Across the room, out the window, over the roads and fields, I sense no movement. Except the rain, which lends the whole outside a pastel hue, as in a painting. I pour coffee, toast a bagel. My eyes wander to the clocks, blinking at twelve. There is no differentiation in light from anywhere in the house, or outside, only an eerie pastel that casts its glare across everything evenly. I call vaguely.

"Hello?"

I become concerned. There is, after all, no one in the house when it seems to me there should be. I drink the coffee, shuddering into the couch and into the silence. Even the dogs do not come when I call them.

"Hello?"

Was that a brief rapping on the windowpane? For a moment, I do not move. Perhaps, I humor myself, I have hopped through a peculiarity in time and my family is in this house but in their time, everyone else's time, wondering where I've gone. In such a state I could continue alone, along in singularity, exclusivity. I open the wine cabinet, dozens of dusty corks peering out at me from their shackles. I pour one, savoring the red rush into the glass that breaks the monochromatic day. The rapping on the window again, this time more urgent. I sway over and swing open the glass door, looking up, and smiling—

"Oh," I say. Oh.

I hold the glass in one hand, the door in the other, and I gape. But I don't move. I don't say, "Well, why don't you come in?" or "Here, have some wine." This is supposed to be my time, exclusively. He is getting wet, hat drooping, glasses sliding down his nose.

Finally, I say, "Okay." And he comes in.

He fumbles with the buttons on my shirt, and I slip off my shoes absent-mindedly.

But you're lost. She doesn't know where she is, the young woman, the girl. She is staring hard at books, at hardwood floors, rushing up to his office ruby-cheeked in expectance. Sometimes he gives you Irish poetry to read while he watches you and you gasp at the turn of every line, and he is duly impressed. If it ever happens, said your best friend, don't tell anyone. And for godsakes, don't tell me.

She watches the rain fall in sheets against the skylight, pounding the glass in quick bursts. The ceiling stares back at her, stark white and judging. There is a knot in the window-shade cord that she wants to unravel, find its hidden metaphor, but as she tries it only tightens. After all, it is not her knot, not her thought.

Afterwards, he sits at the desk by the window and writes. She stays on the bed, pulled into herself, feeling an occasional shiver flit down her bare leg. He has things to tell her, he wants to talk.

The pastel fog begins to rise. I stare out the window and watch as the rain tapers off and a slant of sunlight cuts through the sky just to disappear again, beyond the horizon, when night falls.

Sighted

Colourblind

She said she'd found a system, a way in which it all made sense.

I asked her if it was an order according to colour. She did hesitate then.

She told me: "No . . . according to solidity, the solidity of colour."

"What do you mean, solidity?" I said. I imagined her with those papers disintegrating in her hands. She replied: "Solidity is the gradation of light, the lightness or density of the colour, not the colour itself."

Her brother had once taken me aside to say that she was colourblind, and wouldn't admit it. This was a long time ago. I still don't know if it's true. I guessed it was a sore point and never mentioned it to her. Then I must have forgotten.

It's true though that I never heard her speak of colours by name, the way you'd say, "What a deep red, what a bright blue." She would talk about their *mass* or their *movement*, or about their *beauty* or their *intensity*. I always just assumed we were talking about the same colours. The way we just assume everyone else sees the same things.

She woke me up at two in the morning with her discovery. I hadn't heard from her for over a year. No apologies, no explanations—well, typical. Just that familiar voice, her excitement: "Guess what, I have something to tell you . . ." I listened to her, I actually did. I turned the light back off and listened to her in the dark. I listened to her even though I should have been angry and had a flight to catch that morning. I watched my room gather shape in the night. It's funny, but what she was saying—it comforted me—the way some dreams can comfort you all day. Or maybe—there was this clarity—a clarity beyond the fact that it was her voice speaking—that's why I wasn't angry—I can't explain. It didn't matter who was telling me these things—it just pleased me to listen.

She kept trying to find ways to make me see what she was saying. At night, it was easier to understand.

She said: "It's like a kaleidoscope with no straight lines. Or a map of a thousand unknown countries."

She said: "It's like a landscape, like the desert—you remember that time we slept out in the desert? And the landscape is suddenly fastened to your eyeballs so that everything you look at is part of it."

She said: "It's like snow; it's like the way snowflakes land in winter. Each snowflake lands in exactly the right place. No other place could be more perfect."

"This is important," she had said, and it's true. It is important, though in the daylight it's harder to think about. In the dark, it made perfect sense to me, too.

As she spoke it reminded me of a play—I played this piece long ago—I was still in college. A Sufi play—about birds—well about birds but not really. The bird meeting? The bird conference? Anyway. I had a minor role, a bat actually. And this bat said the most beautiful lines, he said: "I've been flying for years in darkness. I've flown so long in search of the sun that I've come out on the opposite side."

When she told me she had found the sense of the colours, I had to think of this. If she was colourblind like I'd been told, maybe she'd emerged on the other side of blindness.

Lighthouse

There are people—and she was one of them, who can remain so close to you after years of separation, in everything you do, like they're buried in the skin of your palms. And then others, who you see every day, who are familiar out of habit, yet remain strangely foreign, as if they were made from an entirely different substance. I wondered sometimes if she honed in on me from a distance, in sleep. I'm sure she could, if she'd wanted to. Maybe that's why she called so seldom.

She had said finally, on the phone that morning: "I've been circling around this place for years, like a ship around an island, trying to find a port of entry. Now I've set foot in the harbour. The map is unfolding. There is a way in which each thing makes sense. Okay, I'll let you go. Don't miss your plane." Then we hung up. I wondered where she was, and from where she had been calling. And if years ago, when we knew each other better, she had already been circling.

When I met her, she had a small flat on the top of a seven-storey building, with no lift. She had just moved there recently. There was a trapdoor in the ceiling of the one main room, which you could open onto the roof. So she mounted a strobe light on the roof, directly above her sofa bed—she said that she was turning the building into a lighthouse. She made these improbable statements sound completely reasonable. We were nowhere near the sea. I guess she must have already been looking for the coast. "A lighthouse," she said, "is like a reverse camera: mirrors reflect the light, but not inwards, into the black box. Light is reflected outwards, into the night, into the distance. It's said that sailors can see a lighthouse even in sleep."

Each night, she turned on the strobe light, and went out, to circle the building on foot, training herself to navigate toward the place where she slept. She said that the light was visible up to a kilometre away. I imagined her moving through the lamplit streets like a plane coming in for landing. Remembering how to return from a distance.

It wouldn't surprise me if I talked to her more often in sleep than I do waking. I don't remember much of my dreams. But one night, months ago now, she appeared to me in a silver cap adorned with coloured feathers. She was in her attic, surrounded by the coloured papers she was sorting. In the dream I had done something stupid but she had forgiven me. There's a picture I went to look for when I was in Paris again. It's in the Egyptian collection at the Louvre, painted on the side of a coffin. It shows the soul of the dead man, in the shape of a bird with a human head, poised above his own corpse. I thought for a moment: maybe that's what it looks like when she visits me in sleep. Hovering near my bed like a gentle kind of harpy.

Darkroom

Years ago, she had explained the word "darkroom" to me. It was one of her favourite words. My English wasn't so good back then. We hadn't known each other very long. "A darkroom," she said, "is the place where photographic paper is put through a series of chemical baths, in order to bring the captured image to light. *Dunkelkammer*."

"But in English," she told me, "it has a second meaning. It's the darkened room at the back of a gay bar, or a swingers club, where you can have sexual encounters without seeing your partners. The two places are similar. A darkroom is the half-way-house between the visible and the invisible. A place where the unthinkable comes to light in darkness."

I remember thinking, secretly: she's been there. I'm not even sure what kind of darkroom I had in mind. I had a picture of a dark space with a single red bulb. You can just make out shapes in the room, in different shades of red. She had never mentioned that, the colour of the darkness.

I remembered the darkroom not long after she called—the idea appeared strangely hopeful to me. What was it? The *unthinkable*. That was her word exactly. Only something that I could not yet imagine might help me. I decided to build myself a darkroom. I have a guest room in my flat, with a very small window, that I just sealed off. I mounted a single red bulb. I wasn't sure whether to furnish my darkroom like a swinger's club or a photographic laboratory. In the end I just left it bare.

She used to say: "You have to turn your ideas into matter. You have to act them out with your physical body, or make them into objects, rooms, and buildings. Then they can flourish. You should know about that, you're an actor. Ideas that have no physical form are like unborn children—you can't hold them, feed them, or play with them."

When you close your eyes and look towards the sun, everything goes red. It's the colour inside of us, I suppose, of our stomachs, of our eyelids. I don't know if we're blind before birth, but if not this is the colour we would see.

I go into my darkroom in the morning, after waking. Or at night, before sleeping. I go into the room, shut the door, and pretend that I'm standing behind my own closed eyelids. Or beneath my own tongue. Or inside my skull. Or in my throat, or in my gut, or in my lungs. It's quiet there. Nothing is beautiful or unbeautiful, neither bright nor dark. There's just this even redness, over everything—my hands, the walls, the ceiling. I go there alone, like a child playing make-believe. Imagining that I see pictures emerge on the surfaces of unprinted paper, and the skin of unknown bodies.

HELEN CUSACK O'KEEFFE

The Ehrlich Remedy for Grief

Daunted by the rumours of highly eminent patients, Miranda Bittern did not enter the celebrated sanatorium of Lake Davos, but accepted Albertine de Vere's proposal that they take a villa nearby. This scheme would permit the young Bittern heiress to receive twice-weekly visits from Doctor Ehrlich.

Doctor Ehrlich sidled into the drawing room on their first day and seized the hands of his new patient, darting his weaselish black eyes over her slender contours. His great, drooping, black moustache appeared belligerently at odds with his limp frame and his curiously yellow complexion.

"It is very opportune indeed that you have come to Lake Davos, Fraulein Bittern," he announced, "I am so extremely happy to be of service to you." He inclined his head gracefully, so far that the ends of his moustache brushed his collar points.

Miranda extricated her hands from his, finding that her lace mittens appeared slightly damp where his palms had touched them.

"How kind. Do sit down. May I present my companion, Miss de Vere. Albertine, will you please pour us some tea."

The physician's lips rustled under his moustache. "No Fraulein, after such a shock as you have suffered, you should avoid the infusion of pungent leaves, for you it would be utter poison." He waved Albertine's outstretched cup to one side. "As for myself, I consume nothing that does not originate from within an eighteen-mile radius of my sanatorium. Now, for the details of your condition. First Fraulein Bittern, please to inform me, at what time do you retire to bed each evening?"

After asking several more questions, Doctor Ehrlich pronounced a series of instructions that Miranda found comforting for the mere fact of their precision. He urged Miranda to regard herself as a complex, inter-relating system of physical and psychological structures, plagued by enduring conditions of ill-health, which were mostly engendered by the shockingly abrupt death of her fiancé, and by the incapacity of her tender female psyche to cope with such an onslaught. No single diagnosis was specified, neither did Miranda seek one. Given his patient's intricacy, Doctor Ehrlich's directions left no aspect of her environment to chance. Miranda learned that her low spirits must be attended upon with unsparing sympathy, that she must not entertain any emotions that might allow her grief to overwhelm her. In practice, this meant that she should adhere to a diet of boiled meat in bland, milk-based sauces, textureless milky puddings, and a glass of warmed milk before retiring to bed at nine o'clock each evening. Several activities were specifically forbidden: Miranda was not to exert herself outdoors, not to wander the green slopes and forests surrounding the villa, but she might sit beside the lake in the early afternoons, provided she kept herself in the shade and ensured the constant presence of a female attendant. Doctor Ehrlich would personally examine her each Monday, under hypnosis, and one of his special chairs would be sent to the villa for this purpose. Her waking hours should be spent peaceably, she might be read to, but was to avoid troublesome modern stories such as those penned by Monsieur Hugo and his ilk, for they contained too much that would excite the passions.

Certain passages of the King James English Bible were recommended, Doctor Ehrlich having scored through all those that he considered harmful with a large black X. He also provided some improving texts from his own library at the sanatorium, these having been similarly censored. Even a few of Miss Landon's less insipid verses in *The Lady's Book of Flowers and Poetry* had been stricken out by Doctor Ehrlich's wide nib.

"Do you not find it quite astonishing that Doctor Ehrlich has the time to scrutinize all these books?" asked Albertine, after he had left the villa.

"I expect he is a terribly fast reader," replied Miranda. "Do you recall what he said about my laudanum?"

"He said that you might continue with the nightly dose, but that you were not to imbibe it during the day."

"Ah." Miranda looked down at the swirling black bombazine of her skirts.

Obediently, Miranda refrained from reading Hugo and from daytime doses of Laudanum, but she kept her bottles of J. Collis Browne's Chlorodyne hidden and omitted mention of them to the Doctor.

She cared little what Albertine read to her. Her companion attempted to select the least cumbersome of the permitted passages from the Bible, a tome with which neither woman had much familiarity, but after less than a week, these were exhausted. Albertine ventured to read some of the censored Biblical passages, with the caveat that she saw scant literary merit in them. As for Miss Landon's offerings, verses glutinously extolling the virtues of a rose were only amusing the first time one read them.

Miranda submitted to the dull predictability of the Ehrlich-Davos regime with superficial ease, obeying the doctor's strictures to the last detail as she had for years followed the instruction of her governess. Her childhood spirits had lacked any sense of rebellion; her chief sensation then had been of tedium, laced with the vague sense that she would have to make decisions for herself one day. She had never relished the prospect.

Chlorodyne consumption aside, Miranda's efforts to attend to Doctor Ehrlich's commands were met with encouragement, and she found herself wishing to retain a degree of ill health so that she might hold his interest for a considerable period. That was not to say she intended to give the impression that her health had worsened. His Monday examinations under hypnosis left Miranda feeling oddly deflated, but they were not disagreeable.

The celebrated sweet air of Switzerland wafted to and from their throats, whilst the expanse of the lake shifted monotonously at its shoreline, each lazy thrust dabbing and darkening the grey pebbles at the water's edge. The tightly structured lakeside days were so predictable, their tastes, sights and sounds so limited after the thrilling tumult of Paris. The stupor was comforting in a sense, but the lack of stimulation induced brooding. Miranda saw herself in the clutches of tragedy for the rest of her days. She no longer raged at the cruel forces of fate, but acknowledged the idea of a stultified existence. Unenthusiastically, she hollowed out a wretched crevice in which she might suffer for as long as she pleased. It went without saying that those around her, being her socially inferior dependents, should wholly participate in these milky-grey pursuits, just as they donned their black garb for her sake.

Their departure for Italy was postponed, at the insistence of Doctor Ehrlich, who opined that Fraulein Bittern was not yet strong enough to cope with the rigours of travel and the dusty Mediterranean heat. She might consider going there in late autumn, if he deemed fit. He would review her twice a week, with the continued specification that she was to avoid all excitement.

So the faint colour that had managed to reach Miranda's cheeks through the dark parasols and shady pines soon evaporated; her afternoons by the lakeshore were curtailed as the days grew chillier. Certain passages from the Bible became so oft-repeated that they left firmly imprinted but incomprehensible tracks on the minds of reader and listener. The only features of Miranda's daily life unprescribed by Doctor Ehrlich were the gowns she had bought in Paris and her J. Collis Browne's Chlorodyne. This hybrid of morphine, cannabis, and chloral hydrate—intended to alleviate ailments varying from colic to cholera—she swallowed in secret, her elixir seeming all the more effective since she suspected it might be forbidden. Her new gowns, on the other hand, she paraded with quiet triumph, swooping from the terrace down to the lakeside each afternoon, the breezes puffing out the dull, dark folds, her hems slithering silkily over the lush grass.

SION DAYSON

The Idiopath

It is his own sheer luck that he never found himself in the same room with her when the seizures occurred. He didn't know anything about epilepsy and he still doesn't. Something inside him clicked off, or clicked on—he doesn't know which—when she told him. The word itself seemed to mirror a terminal malady, the repeated *p*'s, the *e*'s spitting up on themselves. The seizures would never go away, but recur, a fresh shock each time.

It's a common neurological disorder that can be controlled, she said; he was overreacting. All he could picture were convulsions, him rendered paralyzed, unable to bring himself to reach into her mouth. She informed him this was folklore—people don't actually swallow their tongues. It didn't matter. He didn't want to stay and find out if it was a myth or not.

The doctors say the cause of her seizures is idiopathic—that is, a disorder unto itself. There have been brain scans, MRIs, SPECTs, lasers and machines pointed at her, strapping her in, trying to identify where the problem resides, what's going on inside her brain. She's been trying to tell him what's on her mind, but he won't listen. He's not much of a talker; he's never figured out how to hear what other people say, either.

She had the first one at work. As she recounted it, she had woken up disoriented, having no idea how she had gotten on the linoleum floor, noticing for the first time the bland lime paint peeling at the lower corner of the wall. The antiseptic buzz of the lights confused her. She thinks now it's because they were all crowded into a stuffy room for the receptionist's surprise retirement party and someone kept switching the fluorescent light on and off. No one had ever thought to replace the flickering monstrosity.

The fold-out sofa is damp now; he has woken up leaking absinthe. He didn't shower the night before—foreign city detritus still clings to his skin—and there he is rolling around in sweaty bedclothes that have already accumulated various other bodily effects for several weeks now: come, drool, dandruff flakes. The duffel bag he's been toting across borders is in an ever-evolving state of eruption, spewing forth so many faded socks and T-shirts it stands as a somewhat horrendous installation. It is the most art he's created since he left.

What startled him awake at this hour—4:13 a.m.—is that he had fallen inside a gaping mouth and was drowning in saliva. Now he won't be able to fall back asleep until all the numbers read the same: 4:44. It is one of his peculiar obsessions.

He used to wake up forcefully from dreams a lot—Lisa had learned to live with it—but he had hoped nightmares wouldn't follow him here. Still, sleep has become much more reassuring since he disappeared. Little else is since he left her.

No, he didn't leave her, he tells himself. He added distance. He'd like to say misfortune befell them, as way of pat explanation, but that would be a lie. He loves her, he tries his best. His best is incompetent and selfish. She only had the misfortune of reminding him of what he's tried to forget. He's a coward.

He sleeps heavily when he's been drinking, so he didn't notice before, the incessant honking outside the window, a general noise level, which doesn't seem to correspond to what technically should be the dead of night. At this hour it doesn't seem you could say it is part of the previous night—it's too far gone for that—but it doesn't feel like a new day, either. He often feels displaced in this way—an occupant of fallow space. There seem to be definite realities around him, but he is somehow always outside of them, or precariously in between.

He smells his odor rising off of himself. He thinks about sculpting the unseen, the hidden menace within her. He is thinking again, and that is bad. He wants to drift back toward sleep, but he cannot hurry the clock.

His arm is still tired from lugging all of his crap to the new place—a fifth-floor walk-up, an old maid's quarters. Everything about him feels limp and dull and the last thing he needs to do is spill more semen onto the defeated sheets, though masturbating might relax him. He must do laundry tomorrow. He avoids it even more on the road than he did back home. Even the simplest of duties demonstrate that he is damaged.

He calls her from pay phones because he doesn't have a mobile. No stable landline. More to the point, he needs external constraints. Even the best calling card will not allow the length of time he truthfully owes her; he needs the easy out. *I can't understand what the Italian operator is saying to me, the France Telecom card is beeping, damn these strict Germans, their phone is about to cut me off. I have to go, baby. Talk to you soon.*

"It's time to come home now," she tells him, every time.

His father used to travel for business a lot, but he was very young at that time. The most important aspect of these absences was the presence of his mother. Rose. That was her name. He remembers how the wisps of her long hair would fall into his face as she leaned over to tuck him in at night. He has a memory of a specific scent, too, somewhere between apple spice and Dentyne. It must have been perfume, but he thought it was just the smell of all mothers at the time. How can he make sense of anything he remembers from then—he was five.

His father was somewhere out in the Midwest, a region that still seems to him only an abstraction. His mother had picked up pizza for dinner. She said it would be their little secret. She had to cook healthy meals for the father who already had signs of hypertension even then, but when he'd leave she'd say they were free as the wind and they'd eat fried chicken and hot dogs, anything that left a line of grease on the plates. This was the height of love to him.

He didn't know what was happening. He was only a kid. Did he already give that as his defence? People want to ask him about it and they don't. He doesn't know how to be polite, how to politely tell people he's not about to share that with them. He's figured out that he doesn't have to say anything. He just puts a stricken look on his face. That's not difficult. He *is* stricken when he thinks about it.

Lisa says she's got a device now, right next to the bed. You press a button and the emergency services are immediately notified. It's not necessary—most seizures pass within ten minutes—but she got it to appease his phobias. *Ben, just press the button. That's all you would have to do. Come back.*

He tells her he's in Paris now. He had exhausted his search for the perfect dark ale and, besides, the sound of German was putting him on edge. He doesn't know a word of French, but it is at least more identifiable as language to him than the guttural noises that had surrounded him the past month. He took Spanish in high school just like every other jerkoff who wanted an easy A. He'd smoke up before class and Senor Martinez appeared to think this created a receptive state for learning the melodic rhythms of the tongue. He guesses he'll make it down to Spain after this. If you haven't noticed, he doesn't have a clear path in mind.

He's making his way slowly across Europe, like he's some pimply-faced kid on spring break. He never got to do that when it would have been more appropriate. He was the struggling art student whose dad had cut him off in college—he never had any money. He sold a piece a few years ago in his first solo show in New York. After that, he could shit in a flowerpot and sell it. He's passed somewhat out of fashion, but lucky for him he had never shaken the poor man's dread and continued to live like a squatter, building up a heap of savings.

It's an extended sabbatical, he's saying, checking out the "scene" abroad, looking for inspiration. Really that means he's holing up in tiny studios and drinking himself into oblivion. Trying not to think. Trying not to miss her. Dial tones remind him of her.

His father liked to think of himself as a stoic man. He never said it, *It's your fault,* but his whole manner was that of subtle blame. Why did his father think he needed to accuse? Ben's very good at that job himself.

When the father returned from Ohio, Illinois—wherever it was—he stood in the kitchen, glaring down at him. From then on there always seemed to be a cold draft when they were in the same room together. He hadn't watched as they transferred his mother to the stretcher, wheeled her out into the California evening, too bright and warm. He had stayed in the hallway after calling 9-1-1 like his parents had taught him. When he peered around once, she was slumped over, her whole head bulging out of itself; he quickly retreated back to the passageway.

He doesn't know how those dishes eventually got washed or if the paramedics wiped the food from her face. Somehow it is that small detail he's always attached to as the most disturbing.

Ben suspects the mound of extra cheese on the slice he had been enjoying before she choked looked like congealed wax many hours later.

When he entered the metro on Saturday, he did not at first recognize the sound as connected to anything tangible. He had discovered a local drink and thought the noise emanated from deep within. The taste of Pastis, like licorice soaked in antifreeze, coated all his senses.

As he propped himself against the train door he saw that the noise was actually a man coughing repeatedly, unable to close his mouth before the next cough arrived. As wracking as the sound was, he didn't worry much about it at first—if the man's coughing, he's breathing—but it continued without cessation, steady as a metronome. The man started reaching for the zipper on his windbreaker, zipping it up, down, up, down, like a menopausal woman undecided if she's hot or cold. He rubbed his chest, as if he could smooth out the cough, pat it down. Ben thought of his series, *Cardiac*, left unpresented. All the human organs made of raw meat, spoiling before the gallery opening. He had told them that was part of the intention, but this left no impression.

He was the only person looking at the man. The guy next to him was reading some sort of philosophy text. Nietzsche, Kant. Ben wanted to ask him, *Um, so what do* you *think of this guy here? Seems like he might need some help, don't you think?* But he didn't. He couldn't.

Everyone else—worthless, too. Their nose in a book, newspapers open, tongue down a girl's throat. Ben lived in New York for nine years. He knows how to look at people without looking like he's looking at them, but the people here, they don't even do that.

Aid-ay mwah, see-voo-play. The phonetics from his traveller's phrasebook came to him: What? He was going to say that, then point at the guy? Everyone was aware of the distress and was simply giving the man the courtesy of ignoring his heart attack.

The man started to sweat. Ben too. The man's hand alternated between his brow and his chest. At one point he looked straight at Ben.

The train filled with people, faster and faster. A whole crush entered at Gare de l'Est and he couldn't see the coughing man anymore, but he could hear him. The suffocating feeling that he was the only one paying attention cloaked itself around him. It did not diminish as more witnesses entered the scene.

The man fell out of his chair just as the train pulled into the next station. Ben hurried out and had trouble catching his breath. He looked back and everyone still seemed frozen, uncomfortable with the fact that a man lay at their feet.

He's been riding the line 5 metro incessantly the past few days, hoping to catch a glimpse of the man he's convinced died due to his inaction.

Today there is a young couple sitting across from him who haven't stopped pawing at each other since they sat down. They are in the four-seater and he feels like a giant; people don't seem inordinately small to him here, but the seats do not seem built for the average American male. It is better for his surveillance purposes to stand, but he is so tired, he can't any longer.

Everyone is coughing now; it's catching, like some sort of plague going around. The couple, however, are young and unafflicted. He guesses maybe it's spring.

Earlier today, Lisa screamed at him over the phone. She says his obsessions aren't cute anymore. She asks why he cares more about this random guy than he does about her.

"You want to talk about choking, Ben, I'll tell you what choking is. What you're doing. You shouldn't need a fucking gold star to face up to your life."

Ben didn't say anything, lost in this image, a tiny sticker, a bright golden star.

"You want to know a secret?" her voice growing louder. "We're all fucking afraid. We don't all get the luxury to let that stop us from getting on with things."

She offered a litany of things to be frightened of: falling into train tracks just as its approaching, walking into the bodega in the middle of a hold-up, getting struck by lightning, dying unloved. He could see her point.

The boy across from Ben has reached into his backpack and pulled a piece of paper from it, a charcoal sketch of the girl. It looks worried over and amateurish; it is a completely earnest offering. The girl takes it and lays her hand over her heart for a moment before leaning over toward the boy, a strand of hair getting caught in his mouth as she kisses him. She laughs nervously and tucks the hair behind her ear.

Something in the motions reminds him of everyone at once; the coughing man he's been inexplicably chasing, his mother whose auburn hair smelled like peaches and tickled his nose. Lisa, who had accepted his first sketches of her with humour and embarrassment.

He has a girlfriend whom he's unceremoniously abandoned.

Before he understands what is happening, he is crying. He has been divorced from such an activity for so long that the initial fluid flowing from his eyes strikes him as curious and absurd, but he soon submits to it. He seems unable to quiet the little animal noises he is emitting. If he offends those around him, he doesn't know as everything's turned blurry, the world a watery mosaic.

One of the paramedics back then had told him he had done a good job, asked him if he wanted to ride in the front of the ambulance like a big boy. Ben's father never heard them say that and he's often wanted his father to know. *Tell him, at least I called.* He doesn't think it is enough to tell Lisa that. *At least I call, baby.* In a moment of utter disgust she told him that he was sicker than she was.

Ben is unaware of the impressionable couple's movements or whether passengers have broken the implicit rules and regard him. He gets off the train not bothering to look where he is and stands desolately for a few moments on the platform. It seems to take all his concentration to enact processes that by themselves are unconscious; as if his heart might stop beating if he didn't listen for it, or his spit would spill over if he didn't swallow.

He falls against a pillar and sucks in a large helping of air. He thinks of the graffitied train cars of New York, the underground tunnels like windpipes through which they easily pass. Lisa, whose arms would wrap around him when he'd wake up gasping in their room. He wishes he could turn his brain off, the pictures it conjures, extinguish the seed that lies so buried within that his source of comfort is now conflated with his most primal fear.

Last night, in his dream, Lisa rode his cock, then her head lolled backwards, her eyes rolled up. He tried to get her off of him, but he was stuck, still erect, and her vagina gripped his dick in waves of spasms as the rest of her violently shook. She looked like she was being electrocuted; breasts jiggling wildly. Not arousing. Terrifying.

His breath is calming down as he leans against the pillar for support. He thinks more clinically now, eyes focused on a scampering rat on the tracks: how does one go about disinfecting from the inside? What remains if you rid yourself of yourself? He looks blankly around at his surroundings, realizing he is a disease unto himself. He stands still as strangers pass him on the platform, leaving him, the idiopath, alone.

COLE SWENSEN

Tuning Fork

1
Turning   to the face   to be early
in the east   where a mark   shocks even farther
the gesture, called, heard   and the work hung alone in the cold

but caused no harm   "Everywhere
you turn you see the face of God" (Koran, Chapter 2, Verse 115) heading west
its hands held out as if to brace itself against a fall. Call

and what does it become.

2
Turning   to face   is often too early

a vessel walking—that rife, a river might, a river fall at the slightest touch

he turns. He tries to do it quickly
to be only

and then more quickly   it wandered be
(no other) (empty)

plain upon plain, blindly engraved, and you turned around.

3
Turning, by its very nature, takes place more than once,
is an act enacted upon itself   and there the face
must make its choice.

Poem with the last line cut off in its prime

crows the black a cloud of   of crowds of   that continent there   what
was a continent   they said   we used to have   once there was   a sun
or set   outdid   a sun was once the sill in a small glass with the light coming on
and a crow set all over the sky

Cast-Iron Birds

How odd that they make them
                    (who's *they*?) and why are they not
a contradiction in terms? are
tersed in a swivel,
the yous are a sinew, they too
                              that spiral felled, a forest
heard
where no forest was. but what else is a bird? and if stone can burn,
can burst into flame and the whole house went down. I see
no reason that   and no reason is   all this *yet*

the eye screams on. I unwrapped the box and lifted the lid.
I like contradiction. I like contradictions even more. They burn
straight down, utterly free of gravity.

DANIELLE McSHINE

Grand Palais: *Saint Martin and the Beggar* by El Greco

Coup de foudre
Followed some months later by thunder.
Riveted in front of the painting
Of a man astride a white steed,
She felt the world eddy round her
As it had when she first noticed him
In his jacket and black turtleneck sweater,
Nothing like the aristocratic ruff
Emerging from St. Martin's armour.
And then St. Martin looks nothing like him—
First of all, he is blond and curly-haired,
Tears his green cloak in half
To share with a naked beggar
(Why not all of it? she wonders)—
Yet, she is transfixed by the the elongated limbs
The darkly drawn eyebrows, the dark eyes,
The tender, austere gesture of his head
Tilted downwards,
While lace overflows
From his chest and wrists.
Her head unknowingly mirrors his,
Watching the beggar's face so close to his arm,
So ready to kiss even his iron-clad arm.

Centre Georges Pompidou: *Le violoniste à la fenêtre* by Henri Matisse

Every day, he played a little longer for the sky,
For the open window, for the clear blue light.
He played for the grain of wood, for the oysters' smooth shells
For the filigreed shawls, for the ornate background of notes,
For women's bodies, limber and luxuriant,
Mishandled against exuberant wallpaper,
For clouds shaped like coral, for the view of the sea,
For Picasso's painting in a corner
That troubled him still,
For paper, for a bowl of goldfish mixing red and yellow
For a pair of scissors, for purest indigo.

A Castle for Simone

Simone knows trash from way back when, from before it was renamed litter so decent people would not throw it on the ground. And she knows litter from way back, from before it became trendy—recyclables.

It's the usual, run of the mill family; mother is stitched to the couch and father has glow-in-the-dark teeth. If mother ever gives her daughter's garbage compulsion attention, she says, "Bag ladies aren't made, they're born. I swear when Simone came squirting out of me that child was holding onto her placenta! And let me tell you she would not let go, in no way could we pry open that little grip. It finally dried and shrivelled up. MY GOD! That's when I saw that the unfortunate child had three—three!—eyeballs. Can you imagine *my* pain! And let me tell you—she wailed and wailed for a year until she finally found a scrap of paper on the floor. Since then, I don't believe I've ever heard an additional peep out of that queer-looking child."

But you are a lucky person to have never had the misfortune of meeting father. He's a squarish man as wide as he is tall, with a handsome face and as you know now, glow-in-the-dark teeth. How Simone knows he has glow-in-the-dark teeth, it is best not to say.

Other than the birthmark that resembles a price stamp smack dab in the middle of her forehead and long stringy ears, Simone has vein-shot eyelids, which begrudgingly spread themselves over her three teeny tiny eyeballs. Growing up, thank goodness she was tall for her age with monstrously large hands and arms that came all the way down to her knees—all of which kept other children at bay. Never once, not once as a child, was she made fun of . . . not that she knew about anyway. And I ask you, please do not ever tell her any different.

122 rue St. Vincent is her family's ancestral home. You've probably noticed it on your walks through Montmartre? It sits on the corner of rue St. Vincent and rue Mt. Cenis. Beautiful? Yes, yes you've seen it, the one with carved limestone fes-

toons of flowers with gilded details underneath each of its five-storey windows.

It was there in the eighteenth *arrondissement* where Simone honed her obsession with garbage and the compulsion to pick up stray pieces. As a youngster she thought litter was mysterious: What was it? How did it get there? Had it blown in from some interesting destination, or had it been left there by someone important, like a countess? Yes, Simone put her childhood to good use creeping along the alleys collecting bag after bag of litter.

Late at night, she hid under her bed covers with the day's fresh catch of trash and carefully examined each *objet d'art* by flashlight. Old sheets of newspaper, egg cartons, food wrappers—you name it—Simone found virtue in it all, and was unwilling to part with a single scrap. At first she plumped her sagging mattress with her treasures and then filled the attic and cellar. Running out of empty spaces, she crammed fistful after fistful under the furniture. Soon, all the furniture was raised a foot off the ground, teetering on the garbage pile beneath.

Can you imagine that the stately, respectable home at 122 rue St. Vincent was only clever camouflage concealing a garbage dump? Why didn't neighbours notice its foul smell? Occasionally a tourist passing by would pinch their nose, gag, and race out of sight. Watching them through the window Simone's mother would raise her head up off the couch cushions just long enough to shout out at them, "Idiots!" Simone always returned under her breath, "Normal."

At nineteen years old, she escaped the clutches of her father's glowing teeth and took to the streets of Paris to hunt garbage full time. By twenty-three she had tons of garbage stuffed into secret caches throughout the city, until she met Sara. Having lived most of her life on the streets, Sara is a cardboard origami genius.

"Paper has the best memory," Sara told Simone during her first origami lesson. "It does not matter what you do—open it, stretch it or even iron it—once paper is folded it never forgets that fold. Kinda like people, we never forget our folds do we?"

I am certain Simone probably blushed when she confessed that she'd always had a thing for paper too—but liked it best second hand.

With Simone's debris-hunting talents and Sara's cardboard origami secrets, they built a considerable three-storey cardboard castle for a home at the end of avenue Rachel, secreted away in the Montmartre cemetery. Remember, you and I've been in that cemetery—you spat on the bust of Edgar Degas. Why? Oh yeah, because he would poke his models with hat pins. You're silly really; I mean, everyone is allowed some eccentricities—aren't they?

Anyway, it took months to fold and stack hundreds of cardboard boxes—enough to build a castle. I saw it from a distance once; it was massive, with four turrets complete with armed battlements. Sara even made all the proper origami castle accoutrements: a whole regiment of life-sized soldiers, several ladies in waiting, a moat full of angry snapping alligators, and a slew of hardworking peasants. Sara said there were alligators to protect them, and peasants to tax! She called it a "respectable castle." Simone balked at that, she actually said out loud, "I grew up in respectable, and it was a pile of crap."

For a time they lived a blissful yet not very respectable castle life, until the rains came. Remember when it poured and poured? Well, the water collapsed their splendid castle. Like boats, the hundreds of paper soldiers, peasants, and alligators floated down into the cemetery, flooding the tombstones. But, worst of all, the rains washed away Sara's love. What Simone found out was that sweet cardboard Sara had the habit of finding salvation in a different girl every couple of years. On the day it rained, Sara told Simone that it had become obvious to her that some woman named Mutt offered the only true way.

The day I finally found my sister she was sitting in the driving rain, crying on top of a three-storey heap of wet cardboard. I carried her through the rain, three metro stops, and heaved her up those two flights of stairs. If I had known then that she was going to stitch herself to my couch, I might never have brought her here. To make matters worse, Simone won't admit it, but I think father, with his glow-in-the-dark teeth, is coming over here at night while I'm at work.

MARTY HIATT

Gold

As I returned home one murky Sunday night, alone and hunched into my grey coat, I stopped in the courtyard and beheld my building: each window radiated a flickering glow, as though still in that era that lit its rooms with candles, but for the fact that they danced in all manner of hues and rhythms on the walls and on the faces of the occupants when I could see them. They'd found shelter, their plain profiles told me, and so could afford to sit still and let the colours wash over them until it was time for bed and then work again in the morning.

But from a window on the first floor came a scene altogether different. I saw a husband and wife standing by an empty fishbowl. The warmth of the lamplight contrasted with the evident tension of their expressions. Such a scene would normally oblige the closing of the curtains, but clearly there was no time for that. The wife's eyes anxiously focussed on her husband rather than the bowl. She turned her head to one side and opened up a palm, as though to say, *Are you sure? Can we really do this?* The husband's face was already steeled to the necessity of the task. There was no time for deliberation; there was no time for anything but action. From the liquid package held in his hands he tipped a small goldfish into the bowl. He had done the deed.

The little splash jolted me out of my voyeurism and I moved away in the shadows as the wife came to herself and tried to close the curtains, her eyes darting around in search of possible witnesses. The two then turned out the light and left the room.

I entered the opposite wing of my building and ascended the stairs automatically as the scene repeated in my mind. Two floors up I turned again toward the apartment, as though to reconfirm its presence, and to my astonishment through the remaining gap in the curtains, lit dimly by the light from the next room, I beheld a girl of perhaps eight years in her nightdress padding up to the bowl. She timidly stepped around it, her eyes fixed upon the creature inside. It was just itself, but her eyes could hardly believe its reality: it was another, a substitute, a replacement for something that until now was presumed irreplaceable! Did it dawn on you then, gentle child, that the existence of the being was secondary to its function, which might equally be performed by another, that the end of its existence was not in itself, but in you? Did you have to learn the lesson there and then, without the calming warmth of mother or the secure strength of father's hand on your shoulder as you confronted it?

Her delicate mouth turned angular. There it was: she had the courage to suspect them, they who had ensured she was always sheltered from the harshness of the outside, who had always softened the blows it dealt out or, if possible, received them entirely on her behalf. But this expression was overcome by the pursing of her lips and a slight blush: she was ashamed of her silent accusation, her veracious accusation! She forced it back down; she was renouncing the reality before her, her delicate frame dousing itself in a noxious, silent restraint. Would she just do nothing? Would she continue to present her old self to them, her nature now become an artificial role to be adopted and maintained? The girl tiptoed back out of the room and its glow, never to speak her word. And I, racked by a terrific nausea, struggling for breath, fled down the stairs and back out into the drizzly night.

Exchange

On a sunny afternoon when all the world was at ease, my companion and I sat down at a pavement café just as our discussion of politics and aesthetics was getting interesting. As we sipped our coffees, my companion began to defend his discursive democratic ideal, claiming that in spite of our wretched circumstances we should try to rationally communicate our needs and feelings in an attempt to overcome both our own neuroses and the gulfs that isolate us from our fellow human beings. He defended this idea by arguing that aspiring or even pretending to be fully human was in fact the only means by which we might make possible the realization of humanity.

As he spoke I spied behind him a stumbling beggar bothering some patrons farther along the footpath. His hands were puffed up and clumsy, the nails framed by black lines of embedded dirt. His eyes bulged out of their sockets and lunged at those he addressed. I couldn't catch his words, but his voice burned itself into my memory: bending and slurring, turning upwards, stretching out, cutting short, demented like a passenger plane attempting aerobatics. Those he addressed struggled to ignore the troubling performance: they exchanged cruel small smiles born of uneasiness rather than callousness, or blocked out entirely his presence and brute needs, attempting to push on with their light chatter in the unseasonal warmth. Yet he who lacked civility was indifferent to their discomfort and oblivious to his importuning.

After failing to receive any aid from the others, he approached my companion and, staggering to such a degree that I struggled to distinguish his desired trajectory from the many directions in which his feet tried to take him at once. When he spoke I saw a few lone teeth surrounded by a black emptiness. In a dribbling drawl he gave us his tired lines, being barely present enough to frame his demand as an apology or to enumerate some socially acceptable needs like food or shelter.

Then in a lightning flash the neat, white hand of my companion struck out into the gap between them as he gave his name and asked the other for his. My companion maintained his openness, setting social norms at naught if they risked obstructing rather than facilitating the sympathetic relating of two individuals, hoping that if the man were ever to be treated like a subject he might finally glimpse the possibility of becoming one, and that his approach would give the other patrons pause to reconsider their hurtful timidity.

The homeless man numbly let his hand be taken and vaguely approximated the movement of a handshake, but his leaden eyes swam in his head and he didn't interrupt his harangue to reply with a name. He was ill-equipped to respond to the novelty of propriety. No longer capable of the substantive dialogue that had always been denied him, he sought only his singular goal—he was a mad twin of the entrepreneur, the monomaniac for whom all things are only either a means to the one end or an obstruction of it—namely a lazy dollar that he might put toward the rough wine by which he would obliterate the shame he suffered in obtaining it. He stumbled off, still in the dark despite our sun.

César's *Le Pouce*

At la Défense 6, commissioned by the Établissement pour l'Aménagement de la Région de la Défense.

In a small square ever filling with taxis depositing and picking up hurried businessmen and women stands a twelve-metre-high human thumb cast in bronze. I'm mystified as to the proposal that César would have given for the commission. The only interpretation I could garner from the other viewers was offered by their enacting the gesture itself: it stands for a thumbs-up, they all suggested. In this region of Paris, surrounded by the headquarters of most of France's largest and most powerful private interests, a twelve-metre-high thumbs-up must surely suggest the locker room egotism of rodeo capitalism, a world where cutting a deal is better the more self-interested it is. One's hands aspire to become as hardened as the bronze, the better to weather the exigencies of competitive society and to prevail over the soft. There masculine violence is only barely sublimated into the scoring of economic goals for the firm, whose interests, in spite of the truth, are proclaimed as identical with those of the individual via the bonus he receives for each point scored. And everyone has two *pouces*. The universality of the thumb comforts those who participate in the racket by implying that it is open to anyone with the drive and the get-go, anyone who isn't a whinger or a layabout. But the hardening of the hands of the individual is not a free act, it is obligatory, the price imposed to nourish his organism. The giant thumbs-up, a supposedly universal affirmation, rather exacts universal discipline: it expresses the blind, implacable power that hovers over everyone always, prepared to turn on and squash anyone who hesitates, and, like the police who are its servants, isn't interested in excuses, or in any reality that deviates from the ideal. Whenever reality deviates from the ideal, it is always the fault of the individual, never the institution. We all have thumbs, but we all suffer in the shadow of the Big Thumb alone. Ours are useless to resist. They must rather be put to work post-haste, and at all costs they must not be caught twiddling. But the thumb's universality equally suggests that its power is really nothing but our own, collectively employed, but, in the form of domination, partitioned and distributed to individuals. It is only a big thumb that demands this; not a God, not a machine, not an alien, but something human, organic, which grows and senesces and must always be renewed. The thumb's exaggerated friction ridges highlight this sensitivity, even fragility, in opposition to the chrome and glass of its environs and even to its own material. The suggestion of the malleability of the skin speaks against its own induration, calling to mind a space where such a process might no longer be universally necessary, where the thumb's delicate contours might be permitted to freely develop their sensitivity, to openly and without risk of punishment explore and experience the subtle variations of fine-textured objects and even of other thumbs, gently altering and gently accepting alteration, where the granting of clemency would no longer have to be purchased by a prior callusing.

ISABEL HARDING

Zombie Mermaid

That was the summer they decided to break into people's swimming pools.

The first time they did it was a little scary. Even though Max knew someone who lived in the Pinedale apartment complex, which was how they got the gate code, Meg had goosebumps along her arms before she'd even gotten near the water. It was cooler out than she would have liked, but Max had insisted the weather was perfect for swimming.

He punched in the code and the gate sidled aside for them. The complex was silent, except for the sound of bugs tapping against the orange streetlights in the parking lot. Meg puffed on a cigarette and clamped her hands to the insides of her arms. Max walked ahead of her. He brought up the rusty latch on the gate to the pool area. He held the gate open for her and she padded in her flip-flops to the edge of the pool. There were leaves piled in the corners and dead worms on the bottom. The light in the water mimicked the glow of the TV screens in the apartments above them.

"Well," said Max, "we still doing this?"

"I guess so." Meg took her last drag and tossed the cigarette butt into the water. Then in one abrupt movement she pulled her shirt off over her head and stepped out of her skirt. She jumped in in her bra and underpants, making a splash that exploded off the sides of the complex. She resurfaced and drew in her breath.

"*Oof.* It's *cold!*"

Max was slow in joining her. He dragged his shirt off over his head, and Meg realized it was the first time since middle school that she'd seen him with no shirt on. He'd gained some weight since then. He unbuttoned his jeans with his head tucked down and fumbled with the zipper. Meg wondered if she should say something funny or ironic, but didn't.

When Max was down to his boxers, he stood with his arms folded and looked at her. She smiled at him. Max took a deep breath and plunged in.

"Whoo!" he shouted when he resurfaced. "I can't believe it's still this cold. In June."

"Hey!" said Meg, paddling away from him. "I thought you said it was perfect weather for swimming. You were very convincing."

"I can be very convincing when I'm drunk."

Meg laughed. Her laugh was the laugh of someone who'd smoked far more cigarettes than she had. A gravelly laugh, like an aging starlet from the obscure old French movies they watched now and then.

"So can I," said Meg. "When I'm drunk, or stoned. Or in bed with someone."

Max wiped the water out of his eyes.

"What about when you're sober?" he asked, just as she dove under the water.

She came up, snorting and pawing at her face.

"What did you say?"

"Nothing," said Max. "It was about a side of you I'm not sure I ever want to see."

She squinted at him.

"You're weird."

"You're weird," said Max.

"I know." Meg leaned back and kicked lazily away from him. "That's why we get along so well."

She left him at one corner of the pool where the dead leaves were. He felt fat and pale and chilly. He shuddered and watched her swim along the edge of the pool. He didn't go under again.

When Meg was finished, they got out, put their clothes on, and walked to the Dairy Queen for sundaes. They agreed that their first break-in had been a success and that they would go for something a little riskier next time.

A few nights later Max called Meg to tell her to come over. He'd found something he wanted to show her. Meg had been about to dive back into the novel she was reading and go to bed early. Instead, she changed her underwear and put on her favourite Blondie shirt, an oversized black T-shirt that she usually slept in, and headed down the street.

She and Max had been neighbours since they were kids. They had gone to the same elementary, middle, and high schools, but different colleges. As Meg walked she closed her eyes and listened to the cicadas trilling in the trees all around her. She tried to imagine what it would be like if the sound never stopped. It would probably feel like being trapped inside TV static.

Max's mom opened the door. She'd been watching *Jeopardy!* in the living room with their Dalmatian Bongo, who was too old to get up and greet Meg. Sometimes he grinned at her, baring his yellow teeth and pink-spotted gums. It's just something Dalmatians do, Max had told her once. Meg said it creeped her out.

Meg found Max in his room, a typical boy's room with a bare light bulb on the ceiling and a futon on the floor and laundry everywhere, a Nirvana poster and a photograph of a galaxy Scotch-taped to the wall. Meg never liked to stay in Max's room for too long, although she had to admit he had a better stereo system than hers. When she came in he was sitting in his desk chair fumbling with something in his lap.

"So, what'd you want to show me?"

Max held up the blue ribbon they'd won in the third grade science fair.

"Found it in my closet," he said.

It was the first and only year they'd been on a team. They'd done some experiments with water and food colouring that Meg couldn't recall. She was a little disappointed by Max's find. He'd built it up to be more exciting.

"I was trying to get the hook on the back to work so I could hang it up," said Max. "It was, like, the only time I've ever won anything."

"Then what was it doing in your closet?" Meg asked, but Max didn't answer. He toyed with the hook a little more, muttered, "Fuck it," then took a thumbtack and jabbed the ribbon against the wall.

This time they hopped the fence at the Pineview condominiums. There were spikes all along the fence, but a good distance from the main security gate on the other side of the complex there was another gate that was low enough to climb over. After Max had gone over, Meg swung a leg carefully over the spikes. She'd heard stories about girls impaling themselves and losing their virginity all over again. She tried not to think about them as she made her way over.

They crossed the parking lot to the pool. An unattractive woman and a more unattractive man were making out in the shallow end. Max and Meg stared at them. The couple disentangled themselves and clambered out of the water, giggling. After they were gone, Meg took off her shorts but stayed in her Blondie shirt. It was hard to move around in, like swimming inside a tent. She was relieved when Max didn't ask her why she left her shirt on.

They never wore bathing suits. Swimming in their underwear helped to preserve a sense of summertime spontaneity. Wearing bathing suits would have made it seem like they were trying too hard.

The next time they went swimming, they took a bottle of vodka with them. They drank it as they walked from Max's house to the Pineglen apartments half a mile away. Meg was in a good mood because she'd talked to a boy at a coffee shop and gotten his number. Max's mind was on the Lovecraft-inspired story he'd been working on that day. So far it was only three pages long, but he felt like he'd been slogging through it. He told Meg that writing had been much easier before he went to college. Meg said she knew what he meant.

"You're, like, the only other English major I've ever hung out with," she told him. She was sitting on the edge of the pool, dangling her legs into the water. Max was standing in the water, holding his palms flat against the surface. Meg's voice was loud in the silence of Pineglen. It occurred to Max that *The Silence of Pineglen* would have been a good title for a nineteenth-century English novel. Maybe it had existed once, as an unpublished draft, like his own story.

"You didn't know any English majors in college?" he asked.

"I mean, I knew some." Meg hit the vodka again. "But I mostly hung with, you know, other people. To hear about other stuff. Like art history and astrophysics and dance and shit."

Max wasn't really listening to her. He was thinking how nice she looked in the reflection of the water, all crystally-blue, like in an aquarium. They'd gone to the aquarium downtown once, as kids, just the two of them. It was the first time they'd been anywhere without their parents. He wondered if that qualified as a date. The next time he'd gone to an aquarium, in college in a different city from Meg, he'd been stoned, gotten trapped in the jellyfish exhibit for half an hour, and convinced himself that the exhibit constituted the entire aquarium, until a friend came and rescued him. He'd never told Meg that story. He thought it was too embarrassing.

They never got caught. The security at each complex they broke into was lack-lustre. At most there'd be a cop in an unmarked car that nonetheless looked cop-like, and when the cop had glided off to check out the other side of the complex, they would hop the fence. The gate at Pineglade didn't even lock properly. Pineglade was an assisted living facility.

"I guess they figure everybody's too old and near death to be able to break out of here," said Meg. They were sitting at the edge of the pool after they'd swum for a bit. She lit a joint.

"What if they could, though? I just got chills," said Max, watching her inhale. "Think about all the zombies who must live here. Just walking out that gate."

Meg exhaled a big cloud of smoke in his face. "Man, you're cruel. Calling old people zombies. I fucking love old people."

"You fucking love everybody," said Max, taking the joint from her.

"Not true," said Meg. "I don't love terrorists, or dictators, or animal abusers."

"Really? They're my favourite."

Meg pushed him. He didn't fall in, but took the opportunity to lean in closer to her as he regained his balance. She smelled like the whiskey they'd drunk at his house before they went swimming. Meg took the joint back and looked at him.

"No, but, seriously," said Max. "I think old people are the living undead."

Meg shook her head and took another drag. "That's redundant. You can either be living, or undead. Not both."

"You're so defensive about old people!"

"I just don't see why you're passing judgment on people for something they can't help. Think about when *you're* old."

"When I'm old, I'll know I'm hideous and decrepit and creepy and won't hold it against people if they think so too. I'll feel secure in my creepiness." He puffed on the joint. "When my grandma was really old, like right before the end, she looked just like a corpse. Like a zombie. I swear to God. Just wasting away."

"Stop."

"I couldn't even look at her."

"Please stop."

"I hope I never get like that. I hope they pull the plug on me just as soon as I start to go."

Before he'd finished, Meg stood up, yanked off her shirt, and dove into the pool. For a split second Max saw her nipples poking through her thin cotton bra. He tried not to stare at her breasts after Meg resurfaced and looked up at him in the glacial glow of the pool.

"You look like a fucking mermaid," said Max.

"You look fucking stoned."

"I am." He laughed. "Zombies and mermaids. Maybe I'm hallucinating."

"You wanna get out of here?"

Max was a little surprised when she suggested they go to his house. They walked in silence through the dark neighbourhoods, Meg shaking her hair compulsively through her fingers until it was less tangled. Max wondered if his distaste for old people had turned things sour. He didn't even care about them one way or the other. He was mildly pleased that Meg hadn't wanted to hear about someone pulling the plug on him.

When they got to Max's house, they went to the basement. He had set up a couch and a TV down there to watch movies. He also had a foosball table, but they hadn't played in years. Bongo had eaten all the little balls and the heads of a few of the players.

They watched half of a Godard movie before Meg said she was sleepy and went home. Max tried to read a book but was still too high. He put on a record and after a while he forgot he'd tried to do anything else.

Two weeks later they went swimming for the last time. By then it was early August and the air was already starting to feel different. They went to Pine Forest, which featured a fancy pool with tiles on the bottom, and a lobby like the inside of a hotel, with chandeliers and thick carpet. Meg went inside to use the bathroom. Max waited for her outside and was asked, twice, if he needed anything, which made him wonder if he looked grungy and out of place.

While Meg was on the toilet and washing her hands she thought about the date she'd been on earlier that night with the boy from the coffee shop. He was shy and awkward and had hardly said a word, even though she had plenty to say about college and France and the books she was reading. He hadn't tried to kiss her at the end of the date. She doubted she would try to see him again.

"Maybe he's gay?" she asked Max as they were walking to his house. "Could that be it?"

"Mm," said Max. He was completely sober and clear-headed. Meg had had two margaritas to get her through her date. Much to her dismay, the boy had only had half a beer. She said she regretted not drinking it for him. If she was never going to see him again, it wouldn't have mattered if she looked tacky.

At Max's house, they went down to the basement and sat on the couch. Max didn't turn the lamp on. The only light buzzed sickly through the window above them from the backyard.

"I mean, I don't know what to do," said Meg. She sat at one end of the couch, hugging her knees to her chest. "I thought this boy was cute at first. But after tonight—I don't know." She pressed her fingers against her eyes. "Man, I *need* to get laid."

"I'll have sex with you," said Max.

The dog came in. He walked up to Meg, sat down, and grinned at her. Then he put his head on her foot. He sighed deeply. Meg took her hands away from her eyes and touched Bongo. Max reached out and touched him too, without thinking about it.

"I can leave, if you want," said Meg.

They looked at each other.

"Why would you want to do that?" asked Max. "You just got here."

"Never mind." Meg's face had no expression. She looked at Bongo. The old dog dozed off and started snoring.

"Sorry," said Max. "If that was awkward."

"No," said Meg. "I mean. It's fine. I just didn't know you felt that way."

Max felt like his ears had filled with wax all of a sudden. "What'd you say?"

"I didn't think you would ever—offer. To do that."

"Well, sure," said Max. He felt very warm, like all the blood had drained out of his head and gone everywhere else in his body. "I mean, I just thought, if you're that hard up—"

"No," said Meg. And that was that.

Max turned on the Godard movie where they had left off. After about fifteen minutes of watching and not paying attention, he said, "Sorry," again. Meg laughed, "No, no, no, no, it's *fine*! Really," and to Max, each "no" sounded like a nail being driven into a coffin. Then close to the end of the movie Meg said cheerfully, "But thanks anyway!"

When he showed her out the door, it was two in the morning and the air was thick with August. Cicadas trilled from the trees in the yard, and bugs were flailing against the orange lamps on the telephone poles. Max watched Meg walk down the street. She turned and waved to him. Then she was gone, and he stood alone in the dark. He didn't smoke, but he wanted a cigarette. He stared at the neighbours' doorbell across the street, a tiny pinpoint of light, and became mesmerized for a few moments. He thought about the music he would play when he went back inside.

He called Meg one more time that summer, but she said it was too cold to go swimming, and anyway, breaking into pools had gotten boring. Max started jogging as soon as the weather got a little cooler. He saw Meg at a couple of parties, once with the boy she'd been on the date with. Max went home early and had a dream about a swimming pool, but she wasn't in it.

ELENI SIKELIANOS

Untitled

It is not enough that the buds have come out. It is not enough that it goes a few degrees warmer in the world. The waiter in the park is trying to read my mind. Or is it the garden, is it the water or is it, is it. The little steps through the gravel. Then it is spring, and the tourists have begun to fill up the city like a box of nervous arms and legs. Shout at the top of your compass (sun), dream your dream on that hilltop town I have dreamt before, sometimes I ride my bike. First I go up, then I go down, sometimes I go up or down again. Sometimes there is a town, sometimes a small walled city, sometimes a drugstore and a stoplight to the left. All of it melting or frozen: a milky sun, weak as a dime. Sometimes a small window looks out at an angle on colours (like dandelions carrying their yellows), sometimes I go walking, walking to get there. Then it is spring, and the tourists have begun to fill up the city like a box of chocolates (melting), and as soon as it all melts, men and women are thrown from their seats; and cars shatter. All the voices the city winds up, a crank-up, an off-key box. Where are several thousand seconds? Waiting to collide.

Untitled

Here we are on the Place Saint-Sulpice again looking onto the stone lions who are looking onto the water again. Light plays. I am sitting in the front café and I can't see myself in the glass except when people pass. When people pass they block the light (light plays). I wait for myself to appear. People must pass, and they do with heavy hands and shoes. Your mother says she is never herself in dreams, she only sees herself, but I believe I am never more myself. A dreamer is only an angle of herself in a sliver or a drape. There is a boy throwing a blue cylinder into the air, which he catches spinning on a string tied between two sticks. Your mother says the lions don't look majestic, they just look like themselves. Your mother is sitting next to me even so I write her a postcard on the back of Sainte-Chapelle with a red ceiling, which she says is blue, and stars, experience is a hoax, all the people we speak of, a life moving through the subway elevator or a world, seeing the girl with blonde hair on a stair, another body with his hamster, or TV animals. A dreamer is willing to reflect our most jewel-like and distorted fashions, a sudden walking of the real earth circumstance, that is, over it unto death   The peripteral rows of obsidian pillars around the whole funny jungle   This circumference would not be the animals' shadow but real: real.

The well-tempered clavicle

This is the story of

the boy who almost admits he fell
into the Seine clacking cymbals between two small fingers
about the distance I want to say
between air & air

& the small windows replaced
on the face of the water, the water
was moving toward lights

in a shoulder of tunnel, throwing
sparks off the collar, a swallower
of flames The tiny petticoat throats of the River Look
each pane swallowed frame-by-frame This was written

in The Book of When I was a child I dropped a knitting
needle into the Seine it descended its course under

 bridges & corpses under The Buttresses of Our Lady
of Spiders The legs of the church are
Arachnid, of Barbary, in any old
church of Europe you can hear the voices ascend more

beautiful in repetition when the math was so exact the voices
mixed with the roof

ALEXANDER MAKSIK

Set Me to Sea; Light Me on Fire with Flaming Arrows

We pass beneath cherry trees in full bloom.

It seems too early, but their pink blossoms are bright and wide in the warm March air.

This premature spring is disconcerting. As if this year there's been no winter. It makes me less grateful for the warmth, for the new flowers, the new green.

I'm walking through the Montparnasse Cemetery with my father. Saturday afternoon and people have come to tend to the graves.

We pass a man filling a watering can from a green spigot.

There's a woman with a deeply lined face and ash-coloured hair kneeling before a grave. She's wearing gardening gloves and plucking dead petals from a small planter.

My dad and I walk and point out graves to one another.

This one is garish.

This one holds Baudelaire.

There's Ionesco

Sartre and de Beauvoir are buried right through here.

There's a sculpted cat atop a low slab of black marble.

No name. No dates.

"What are we to think?" My dad asks. "Big grave for a cat."

I imagine a forsaken woman.

But why must it be a woman? Why can't I imagine a lonesome man?

I should imagine myself.

There's a woman bent at the waist. She's arranging flowers on what I assume is her former husband's grave.

She moves the pots with a worried expression. She squints at the flowers and speaks absently to a tired-looking man in a black suit who holds a small open bag of soil.

This must be her son.

I imagine they come together every Saturday to take care of the flowers.

To wipe away the rainwater.

The man's a bit older than I am, his hair pushed back, covering a bald spot. He watches the sky and keeps the soil far from his suit.

As we pass I catch her eye.

"*Bonjour*," I say, but she doesn't see me, doesn't hear.

We pass a man holding his worn brown corduroy jacket across his knees. His eyes are closed, his head tilted to the sun.

Throughout the cemetery it's like this. People enjoy the day. Tourists look for dead celebrities.

Families replace dead flowers with fresh.

A woman sets her shopping bags at her feet. They're full of groceries. Bruised yellow squash.

Lemons.

She's wearing a knee-length skirt bending stiffly, brushing dirt from a rose marble headstone.

"I wouldn't like to be buried," I tell my father.

"No, me either," he says.

"I like the idea of a Viking funeral," I tell him. "Set me to sea; light me on fire with flaming arrows."

"Or an Eskimo funeral," he suggests.

"An Eskimo funeral?"

"They lay you on a chunk of ice and send you into the ocean."

All around us are high modern buildings. The hideous Tour Montparnasse rises insolently to the west.

Along the rue de la Gaîté artless concrete buildings bear down.

We pass a grave with two tall, interwoven, bronze hands.

"A bit much don't you think?" My dad asks.

They're familiar to me, these hands.

When I first moved to Paris I was in love with a girl. On a very cold day, my first winter in the city, the two of us walked through this cemetery. We took photographs of the hands.

We thought they were beautiful then.

They seem less so now.

"A bit much," I say.

"The thing about not being buried is that no one can come and visit you," my dad says.

"I'd like to be cremated," I say. "Scatter me somewhere. Build one of those memorial benches. Somewhere beautiful where someone can come and sit."

"Yes," he says. "That'd be good. I'd like that."

We stop in front of a grave that's crowded with offerings. There's a piece of cake. Toys. Flowers. A small Buddha. A couple's been buried together. Both of them died younger than I am today.

When we turn away I feel something hit my shoulder.

A bird's shit on me.

We laugh. Good luck. Bluebird of happiness.

He gives me his cloth handkerchief.

He's the only person in the world I know who carries a handkerchief.

At the gates of the cemetery we find a spigot. I dampen the cloth and try to clean my shirt. It's hard for me to see, I struggle, but I can't get at it.

My dad gently pushes my hand away, his fingers briefly touching mine.

He takes the collar and dabs at the stain.

He does this over and over until it is nearly gone.

When we leave the cemetery there is only a faint yellow halo on my collar, barely discernible in the fading afternoon light.

ALICE NOTLEY

An Interview with Alice Notley
by Megan Fernandes

I was late to meet Alice Notley for our interview. When I emerged from the stairs of the metro, I saw a figure waiting on the street. My first reaction was how beautiful she looked, tall and delicate, her hair wind-swept and her small figure huddling into a black blazer in the chill wind of Paris' ninth *arrondissement*. We *bised* and let out a short laugh, I think both of us looking at each other with awkward expressions. As we walked to the café near the metro Cadet, we chatted lightly. She had very kind eyes.

Two things struck me throughout my interview with Alice Notley. The first is that she has a range of laughters. In some of her laughter was an enormous emotional investment, a deep and generous sing-songy boom. Some sounds were bare trills, cackles, and others had real projection and force especially when she would talk about her childhood or fellow poets who had passed away. Often she sang or gave her opinions with intense energy, and just as often she was quiet, distracted, and shy. Her best laughter was when she laughed at herself, engaging in a self-dialogue of whose aesthetic she has mastered in her own work. I also noticed that Alice was very generous and forgiving of a clumsy and self-conscious academic. To be truthful, I felt quite young interviewing her, and I soon abandoned my pages of prepared questions when I realized that no amount of researching the critical reception of her work was going to get us anywhere. Alice wanted to talk about poems and poets. She had a real ear for conversation, and was thoughtful and direct with her answers, though she was not afraid to wander. I did not realize this until I began transcribing our interview, which I think demonstrates her voice and the unexpected movement of her storytelling.

It is with regret that I cannot share the entire interview in this anthology, but it was both too long and had some especially sensitive moments best left unpublished. Even so, what is presented here is some rewarding insight into the mind of Alice, who talks about her family, her fellow poets such as John Ashbery and Robert Creeley, the "diseased" MFA programs, her struggle with hepatitis C, and of course, her personal experience of Paris.

Megan Fernandes: How has living in Paris allowed you to write about a broad spectrum of American culture?

Alice Notley: I came here in 1992 and, oh, that question is just too big! (Laughter.) The first thing I wrote when I was here was a poem called *Désamère,* and it is actually this fiction that takes place in a large global warming desert. The first thing that happened when I came here was that I faced the problem of global warming because I was completely cut loose from my secure place, which was a little apartment in NY on St. Marks Place, so I wrote this story about global warming. Within it I was trying to fix myself in France so I used metrics, forms derived from Marie de France in the late medieval period and early Renaissance.

MF: How long were you writing *In the Pines*?

AN: I wrote *In the Pines* in 2003–2004, so that's over ten years later.

MF: And you just published this in 2007?

AN: Yes, there is always a gap. And it is written under entirely different circumstances. I was doing the cure for hepatitis C and the whole book was written while I was doing this eleven-month cure. And it takes place form start to finish within this cure period. Since I've moved to Paris, I've written *Désamère* and after *Désamère,* I wrote *Mysteries of Small Houses,* which is a series of autobiographical poems that are arranged in the form of chronology and autobiography. They are essentially trying to figure out what the self is, everybody was using the word "the self," the phrase "the self" at that time and I couldn't figure out what they meant so I decided to do an investigation, but what I ended up investigating was my own interior history because that was the only thing I had, that's the only thing anyone has actually to investigate, in my opinion. So I wrote this book *Mysteries of Small Houses,* which won some awards and was nominated for the Pulitzer Prize, rather surprisingly. And then I wrote *Disobedience.* And *Disobedience* is actually about being here, it's about this big strike, the *grève* of 1995 and the events around that. And what it felt like to be in Paris during the time when the city was in a state of upheaval, there were a lot of bomb scares, the Algerians were setting off bombs here and there. I started the book and I was trying to record certain things about what it was like to go along from day to day and then at a certain point there was this huge three-week transportation strike here. You had to walk to get anywhere for three weeks.

MF: All the metros and RERs?

AN: All the metros, all the buses. So my husband couldn't get to work. Every day it took him an hour and half to walk to work and an hour and a half to walk back. To get to the library, which I was using quite a bit then, I had to take an hour-and-fifteen-minute walk. And that sort of set the poem off on a kind of trend where I was discussing French politics and American politics and the Americanization of the world and globalization and whatever I was picking it up in the newspaper and sort of connecting it with what was going on in my psyche. And I was recording my dreams at the same time.

MF: When you say you were recording your dreams, you mean you would wake up and try to document them?

AN: I would wake up and sit up in bed and I would write down my dreams and then I would decide whether or not to put them into my poems. And sometimes I did and sometimes I didn't.

MF: Do you often have trouble sleeping? Because a lot of the poetry seems to be about sleep anxiety or dream speech.

AN: I write a lot about dreams. I write a lot out of dreams. And I am very interested in the differences between sleeping and waking and writing poetry. Poetry seems to exist somewhere between sleeping and waking, it's in this other place. And then there is the place where you make a story out of, either imaginatively or out of your life, there is some story taking place that's in all of us. I was trying to put all those places together in *Disobedience*.

MF: How do you feel about the critical reception of your work in academia? Do you feel like it is completion of the reading?

AN: Oh, I want to have it. Anyone wants to have it. I don't care what they say exactly but I want them to do it. That's what they are supposed to do. They are supposed to figure out what is valuable. Academia . . . I think what academia does is essentially conservative really; it conserves things. It's supposed to decide what is valuable to the extent that it can and then save it, point its finger at it. That's what it is supposed to do. And teach it. And I want to be part of that. But I don't want academia to teach poetry writing.

MF: So, MFA programs?

AN: I came out of one but I think there are too many and I don't think necessarily that they are a very good idea. There can't be *that* many good poets! (Laughter)

MF: Alice, I was just at the John Ashbery conference here in Paris. There was a lot of discussion of Ashbery's astonishing vocabulary, and I was wondering if you also have love affairs with certain words that keep resurfacing in your work?

AN: I have a love affair with John Ashbery's vocabulary, but I don't want to tell anyone about it. I don't know about my own. I am not sure what words I use over and over, but I probably would not want to be reminded (laughing). Everybody has these little reflexes, these little word reflexes. I think John keeps word lists.

MF: Word lists?

AN: Oh yeah.

MF: Well, he does seem like a meticulous guy.

AN: He keeps word lists and title lists. He often starts with the title.

MF: I heard he is an object collector, which I did not know. I just found that out at the conference. Someone quoted him saying: "The American vernacular is an important stimulus for me." Do you find that true for yourself?

AN: It can be. John takes words, he finds whatever is current. Some of the words he uses are really terrible and then he makes them into a surface and it is just an entirely different process from what I do. I have an ear for the way people talk and I am more interested in something like a curve or an intonation pattern or something like that. It is more musical than word studded. I am not inside it anymore, I am here (Paris). John was here when he was very young and the work he wrote here was very different because he had lost his connection with the American idiom and I, in part, have lost mine as well. I do some other things since I have been living here for seventeen years almost.

MF: What is your opinion of the anglophone writing community here?

AN: Well it changes all the time because hardly anyone is permanent and that's a problem. I mean if you are permanent here then it is hard to have permanent connections inside the anglophone community. That's always been a problem for me, and sometimes it is very taxing.

MF: Do you run workshops often in Paris?

AN: No. For some years I did one with my husband, and, uh (laughing), I ran out of things to tell them, I think. Also, I take a lot of trips now so it is hard to do something continuous.

MF: Do you consider yourself a self-conscious poet? I am thinking of Robert Creeley when I ask you this, and how critics having described him as "stumbling" into a poem.

AN: Well, Bob would talk his way into the poem is what he would do. Then he would read these poems with these marvelous line breaks. And if you read the poem for yourself the line breaks are discovered to accentuate emotion. They are really emotional, really. I don't think anyone has talked about this adequately. He was a good friend, and I could never quite figure out how to be influenced by him. Towards the last years of his life, I already knew that it was not only possible, but that I had already been influenced by him.

MF: Who are some of your favourite living poets today?

AN: I'm my favourite living poet.

MF: That's a good answer.

AN: I don't know how many poets would say that, but it is certainly true for me. I'm my favourite living poet.

MF: Are you still dabbling in the visual arts?

AN: Yeah, but it is hard to do because I don't have enough space here. I only had enough space once when I lived in Chicago, and I had a room of my own. Here, I have a very small apartment. I'm a collagist and I can't find enough garbage here. I can't find enough garbage and I can't find the right garbage.

MF: You should try living in Santa Barbara, California. You can't find any garbage there.

AN: I know Santa Barbara a little. I know what's its like to go there.

MF: It is like Disneyland.

AN: Yeah, it is pretty though.

MF: One thing I noticed in your poetry is that you use a lot of personal pronouns, prepositions, and conditional statements. In fact quite a few of the poems in *In the Pines* have verses that begin with the word "If."

AN: Can you point one out to me?

MF: Sure! This is one of my favourite poems in this collection, "Dialogue in the Glass Dimension."

Alice begins reading the poem out loud.

AN: See, this is Creeley-esque, but it isn't deliberately that, it is an accident. But I wouldn't have known how to do it if I hadn't known Bob, and it is very different from other work of mine. I was using a Korean form in this poem and there is a book called *The Korean Singer of Tales* and it talks about these Korean dramatic forms and there is a measure, and I approximated the measure as it is outlined in the book. And it involves breaks in the line and I used that to write the poem. I wrote this when I was very upset because I was doing this treatment, this medical treatment, and I didn't know if I would survive. And I am discussing what it is like to have been myself, to have been formed by society, etc. It's abstract but it isn't really. It is very emotional, but I'm pulling back all the time because I don't want to do it. I don't want to go through it, but I do because that is what you do onstage, I think. It is like a dramatic performance.

MF: Do you feel like each of your poems has its own voice?

AN: Yes, they are all musical and dramatic.

MF: Are you still writing epic poetry after *The Descent of Alette*?

AN: I wrote that before I left New York, and also *Disobedience* is very long. I just had a book come out last week. It is called *Reason and other women* and it is very long, but it's not in epic form, it's just a longer form. I seem to only write these long things at the moment. I wrote *Reason and Other Women* in the late nineties and there is a book called *Alma* or *The Dead Women*. Those are the ones I wrote about

Doug's death, 9/11, and the Iraq war. Everything happened together—it was all my grief, all mixed up with politics.

MF: One thing I also wanted to note is the way in which you use very abstract language, like "one" or "thing," and you make it meaningful.

AN: I often have to go to stripped-down language in order to be logical, but I do other kinds of things too. I am a user of pronouns, like if I read for you from the title poem, I feel like you would hear a completely different voice. Have you played any tapes of me reading from it?

MF: Not from *In the Pines*, I don't think there are any from that collection on the Internet yet—only from *Grave of Light*, *The Descent of Alette*, and . . . well, you've written more than twenty-five books, so it's hard to keep track! (laughing). Do you see a return to mythology in poetry?

AN: Oh, I always go back to it. Then I pull away when I get a new idea, but then I go back to it. Are you attached to any mythology yourself?

MF: The Psyche myth. I also know a poet who is doing some work on the Persephone myths, which has been very intriguing for me. Other writers in this collection, in particular Eleni Sikelianos, wrote an essay about you in a book entitled *Women and Influence,* and a lot of young poets included here cite you as a major influence on their work. They have often discussed your philosophy of the line, which seems to make your work permeable. I don't know what your thoughts are about that or how you make decisions about line breaks and pauses. How deliberate are those choices?

AN: Well I tend to be under the spell of something in each work. You picked out the one word in *In the Pines* that is not connected to folk song. Most of the rest of the work is connected to folk songs, except that there are these stories, stories of pure prose. If you heard me read from another part of the book, then you would hear that song. There are only two that are connected with the Korean form; there is the one we read and the last poem in the book, "Beneath You." There are a couple different kinds of poetic forms that I invented out of folk song. *In the Pines* juxtaposes the long line with the short line, and then there are some shorter poems that are like songs, and then there is this other longer piece, "The Black Trailor," which is this Mexican song, "El Preso Numero Nuevo," and it is about this guy who killed his best friend and his wife. He is about to be executed and then this priest comes to his cell, but the guy doesn't regret killing them and says when he gets to the afterlife, he is going to look for them and kill them again. (Laughter.)

MF: That's quite a long poem, isn't it?

AN: Well, yes, it's more like a story, but when I read it aloud, it sounds like a poem.

MF: Do you see a return to narrative now in poetry?

AN: Well, I returned to narrative, but I didn't ever go through language poetry. I started out as a fiction writer. I went to Iowa's workshop for fiction. I met some poets and so I changed to poetry, but I was always going back to fiction techniques. In my earlier work, I used mostly dialogue. I used dialogue and story shape, and then gradually I learned how to tell a real fiction story. I've been doing it ever since, and it's very hard for me not to.

MF: How did you come to the decision to write *Alette* as an epic? Is that something you have always wanted to do?

AN: I wanted to do it because it was considered to be the epitome of Western poetic achievement and only men had done it. And because it was ancient and no one was thinking about it anymore, except in the way Pound and Olson had done it in modernist terms, and I thought post-modernism and post post-modernism were all passé. All the post posts were boring and everything was fantasy, I think.

MF: You said earlier you never went through language poetry, and I have a quote from another interview where you said, "The young generation of poets have survived the 'factualism' of language poetry."

AN: Yes they survived all the poetry groupings and all the movements, but it is slightly diseased by the MFA program and so I don't know where it's going to go next. Are you in an MFA program?

MF: No, I'm not. I'm a PhD student.

AN: What do you do?

MF: When I started my PhD, I came in as an Irish modernist. Now my interests are expanding it seems.

AN: Oh, so you're a scholar. Do you write poetry?

MF: Yes, but that has been a rather slow development. I come from a very science-oriented family.

AN: Well, I did it because I was trying to figure out how to be a writer, and I had no idea what to do about it, this urge to be a writer.

MF: Was your time at Iowa useful for you?

AN: Yes, because I made contacts. I think I went there to figure it out, but you can do the same thing by going to New York. The key thing is having a community. I met my first husband Ted Berrigan there. Actually, I met a lot of people there.

MF: How long were you married?

AN: I was married to Ted for thirteen years. Then I was a single mother for four or five years, and then I married Doug Oliver for thirteen years. I have one grand-child and several step-grandchildren, and my two sons have books published. My son, Edmund, also has some CDs. He is a musician and plays guitar.

MF: Do you feel like they are very influenced by your work and your voice?

AN: We lived together inside this poetry community and they are still inside it. I am not really inside it anymore; well, I am to the extent that I can be, but not as much.

MF: Do you teach at Naropa?

AN: Oh, I go there for a week. I don't teach anywhere. I don't do anything. I have no money.

MF: Really? But you've published twenty-five books!

AN: (Smiling) I know, but you don't make any money.

MF: Tell me about your experience with your publishers. You've been with Penguin and Wesleyan Univerity Press.

AN: Yes, and I have another book coming out next year with Penguin, but as they tell me, you can't sell more than 3,000 copies of poetry books in the US. That's the ceiling. And you get a few thousand dollars in advance, and you get royalties. And they will keep your book in print. They are actually very good. People in the avant-garde world put them down, but I think they are excellent poetry publishers. But they can only do a book of mine every three or four years.

MF: How do you feel about 3,000 books of poetry being the ceiling in the US?

AN: It's ridiculous. It's really ridiculous. People don't know what poetry is. They have no idea, and the way it is taught in high school is stupid. The poems are so divorced from the voice. It is taught this way in colleges too.

MF: You think the students should listen to the poet reading the poetry?

AN: Yes. They should make contact with concepts like sound, metrics, whatever is being used, but poetry is about the voice. Every poet has a different voice.

MF: I remember reading Robert Creeley's "I Know a Man," and after a while I finally listened to a recording of him reading the poem and it completely changed how I felt about the poem.

Alice recites "I Know a Man," laughing and imitating Creeley's voice.

MF: How hard is it for you to read some of your work? In particular the poems about your husband?

AN: It can be very hard to read, although when I was writing them, it wasn't. And I wrote most of those poems in Paris, some in Needles, California, but mostly in

Paris. I read them around places here, and it was part of my grieving process and now it just kills me to read it, but also the poetry is just difficult to read. There are a lot of words on every page and to remember the musical structures of each poem—well, they are very individual.

MF: Even *In the Pines* has a different musical structure for each poem, correct? Do you really have to prepare for your readings then?

AN: Yes, but I have a tendency when I am working on something longer to read it out loud at night. I build up the sound inside me, so I don't have to rehearse a lot.

MF: And what about your revision process?

AN: I cut a lot. I almost always cut at least a third.

MF: Do you find your writing process is different depending on where you live? Paris versus Needles or New York? Such as *In the Pines*?

AN: I wrote the first poem of *In the Pines* and I realized it was really good, and I wasn't going to write anything else like it for some time. And then I wrote that long work, which really devastated me, but it came from nowhere. I think a lot of it just came from nowhere, but I was sick. I was doing this hepatitis C treatment and I had to give myself injections and take pills every day. And the injections made me really sick, and I was just sitting in this chair all the time being really sick, but I could write.

MF: And this was in Paris?

AN: Yes this was here. It (*Pines*) is a very depressed work, but my son Edmund would send me a lot of CDs, largely Bob Dylan singing in concert. And there were these different versions of two or three key songs. One song was "Black Jack Davy," and one song was "Blind Willie McTell," and those two songs permeate the work. And "Man in the Long Black Coat," and there was also the title song as sung by Leadbelly (Alice begins to sing) "Black girl, black girl, don't lie to me. Tell me where did you sleep last night." (Laughing) I would listen and I would write and the songs occur in the work. I misquote from them a lot.

MF: How has your sickness influenced your body of work?

AN: I cured myself. The treatment cured me of the virus. My liver was on the verge of cirrhosis, but then you regenerate. I stepped back from the edge of cirrhosis. I was getting checked for cancer a lot, but now I am only getting checked once a year. That's why I live here, because of the healthcare. I know in the United States they are supposedly passing this revolutionary law today, but it's a total jip. It's a total gift to the companies.

MF: Do you have any family here?

AN: No, I don't have any family here. It is lonely here.

MF: Have you ever considered writing a memoir? Do you think your poetry functions as a memoir in any particular way?

AN: To the extent that I am interested, I think my poetry functions as that. I hate prose though.

MF: Really? Why is that?

AN: Because it gets all the attention and it's not as hard to write as poetry.

MF: I suppose it certainly feels more accessible to people, particularly students.

AN: It has too many words. Poetry can do everything prose can do, except make you feel relaxed in that particular way. I read a lot of trash. I read genre literature. I read detective fiction all the time in two languages. I've been doing it since I was twelve.

MF: How do you feel about your poetry being described as feminine or exploring feminine consciousness?

AN: I find that a bit difficult, because I don't think that things should be divided into feminine and masculine. On the other hand, what's been associated with women has been ruled out of all power structures so it has to be *named* somehow. But I don't feel particularly feminine.

MF: How has dialogue been important in your poetry?

AN: I can divide into characters, and I can make characters out of several people molded together. I can do fiction tricks, collage tricks.

MF: And how did you make the selection for *Grave of Light*?

AN: You know, I cut out a lot. I continuously cut out my earlier work, I really need to publish a collection of my earlier work. I found myself making a story in the book. I found myself trying to make it a good read, as if it were a work of fiction. I wanted the reader to be able to read it from cover to cover.

MF: Is that how you read collections of poetry, from cover to cover?

AN: I don't read much poetry. I do weird things with poetry right now. I read bits and pieces and I read lines and words and I read things like books of Latin and Greek prosody. I read prosody. I keep trying to teach myself Greek and I scan prosody for sound. The only poet that I have been reading consistently who is alive is John Ashbery. I've been reading his past five or six books, his old age works, but I'm not sure I'm actually reading them. It's more like I'm getting them telepathically (laughs).

MF: Do you mind reading some work from *In the Pines*?

AN: Sure.

Alice Notley reads from Section 5 of In the Pines.

MF: Was that hard to read?

AN: Uh (pause) no. I just had forgotten what it said, I had forgotten. I wonder why I don't read that one out loud.

MF: If I may ask, how much of this is autobiographical?

AN: Well, it's hard to say because I'm doing something in that work, I'm taking a lot of people and calling them "he" and "she." Their stories are all melding because I'm not naming anyone. I am being poetical and elusive and telling a story about telling, but it's all true.

MF: Just untraceable.

AN: Yes, probably.

MF: When you go back and read something you have not read in a long time, do you see through all the ambiguities and gaps, or is it also untraceable for you?

AN: Sometimes, but that one I knew very well, I just hadn't read it in a long time. The title poem took me two months to write.

MF: Do you often use this question and answer method?

AN: Yes, I probably use it too much. There was a kind of work that I started writing in the seventies where people ask each other questions all the time and answer them. There was a lot of repetition, and juxtaposition. There is a basic image that keeps coming back in the work and that is of a man in a bed with his eyes on fire. And that is an image that I saw at one point and I kept returning to. It was my father essentially.

MF: Did he encourage you?

AN: I think he liked it, but he didn't know how to talk about it. My mother is very proud.

MF: Are they writers as well?

AN: No, they ran an auto parts store. (Laughing) I'm always writing about auto parts; I find them very suggestive.

MF: There is quite a lot in your work that responds to war. Can you comment on this?

AN: My brother was a Vietnam vet, and he was very tormented. He died of an accidental drug overdose in 1988. He had very severe post-traumatic stress disorder. I guess I am trying to save him.

MF: Some of the other writers included in this volume, such as Barbara Beck and Eleni Sikelianos, have mentioned that you have been enormously influential since you came to Paris in 1992, particularly in your use of the fragment.

AN: I wasn't deliberately trying to do anything with the fragment. When I came here in 1992, I co-taught a workshop at the British Institute with Doug Oliver. We represented two kinds of poetry together, American poetry and British poetry. We also co-edited a magazine called *Gare du Nord*, which was a terrific magazine that published work from Britain and the United States, but it was part of our home, which was near the Gare du Nord, a place where the train came in and the Eurostar had just started up. We represented two possibilities in poetry and we melded them. We argued a lot in class, and everyone really liked that.

MF: What do you mean when you say British and American possibilities?

AN: Well they are two different languages! Two different types of English. There are a lot of ways to speak French, for example, but also a lot of ways to speak English and now there is Australian, Canadian, Irish, etc. Most of my students were American, English, and French, but it was a pretty international workshop. Some people decided they could write in English, but they couldn't. But I found it all extremely interesting. One foreign girl wrote all in English because she could only place her imagination in a foreign language. There were a lot of fiction writers in the group.

MF: Are you still living by the Gare du Nord? How do you find that area?

AN: Well it is very mixed. I live in Little Turkey, but there are so many who live in that area. Indians, Africans, etc. I've lived there since 1995.

MF: And where do you write in Paris?

AN: I write at home, but I do go to museums. I get something out of museums.

MF: Do you attend any of the poetry readings here in Paris?

AN: Yes, I go, but the language of this city is French and the poetry of this city is French, and I'm an outsider and I will always be an outsider and our scene is an outsider's scene. I get a lot out of being an outsider. I see the United States very clearly from here, but I still don't understand enough about French culture and French politics. It is a very mysterious culture to me. The race relations have become much more subtle here than they used to be, they are becoming more and more interesting and complicated. I think it's because the French are anthropologists at heart. (Laughing) They are never really against you, but they are studying you.

MF: You feel studied?

AN: After ten years in my neighbourhood, I realized that people knew me, and that they were watching me, and that they were watching over me. When I got sick, people that I didn't know, but knew in an everyday way, they cared about me. I used to be very shy in French, it's my big problem in French. Now, I like to talk, it is the main thing I like to do. The French are really weird about poetry now, they think everything is poetry except poetry. There is the poetry of this and the poetry of that, but poems are *not* poetry.

BIOGRAPHIES

Suzanne Allen's poetry has also been published in *Nerve Cowboy, Pearl, California Quarterly, Cider Press Review, Spot Literary Magazine,* and *Not a Muse: the inner lives of women,* a world poetry anthology by Haven Books. She lives between her native Southern California and Paris, France, where she directs the Creative Writing and Literature Program at WICE—a nonprofit organization providing cultural and educational programs for the international community.

Mia Bailey was born in 1975 in Bangkok, Thailand, and is Australian and German by nationality. She grew up in Australia, Canada, France, and Japan, studying in Australia, the UK and Germany. Currently she is working as a visual artist in Paris, France; Basel, Switzerland; and St. Blasien, Germany. Her work has also been recorded as part of the video installation *Sighted* and forms part of a larger body of visual and written work.

David Barnes moved to Paris in 2003 with the idea of staying for six months. He is still there. He won Shakespeare and Company's short story competition, Travel in Words, in 2006 and now runs a writing workshop there and a weekly open mic poetry night in Belleville called SpokenWord (http://spokenwordparis.blogspot.com). His stories and poems have been published by *Spot Lit Magazine, Upstairs at Duroc* and *34th Parallel.*

Barbara Beck is an American poet and translator who lives in Paris. She has been the editor of the Paris-based English-language journal *Upstairs at Duroc* since 2002. Her work has appeared in *The Los Angeles Review, Van Gogh's Ear, The Chariton Review, Poetry Australia, The Literary Review, Slightly West, In'hui, la dérobée, L'étrangère* and online at *ekleksographia.* She has published several books of poetry translations, the latest of which is a collaborative translation done with French poet Dominique Quélen of *Livingdying* by Cid Corman, published as *Vivremourir* by L'Act Mem in 2008.

Edward Belleville is completing an undergraduate degree in English and French at the University of Leeds, following a year of teaching in Paris. He has had the opportunity to study with poets Vahni Capildeo and John Whale and has been published in *Poetry and Audience*, one of the longest-running poetry magazines in the UK. His next project will be based on a recent two-month trip through Africa, and while he is no longer a resident of Paris, the city's influence has been formative—one to which he returns frequently if not bodily.

John Berger is a storyteller whose novels include *G* (which won the Booker prize). You can read his discussions about writing, art, and much else in *And Our Faces, My Heart, Brief as Photos*. The story printed here is an extract from *Here Is Where We Meet* (Bloomsbury, London, 2005. Pantheon, NY, 2005). Born in 1926 in London, he has lived in France for many years.

Judith Chriqui graduated from Sarah Lawerence's creative writing program in 2009. She has written music reviews and for *two.one.five magazine* and is a current contributor to various online magazines and travel blogs. She has lived in Paris, Philadelphia, New York City, and currently resides in Tel Aviv where she is working on her creative nonfiction.

Marie Davis is a novelist and internationally syndicated cartoonist. Her humorous audio novel is *Hey Diddle Diddle—A Naughty Delight for Lesbians and Other Grownups* (MotesBooks, 2008). Her short story "The Million Dollars I Won and Ate" is included in *Motif: Come What May* (MotesBooks, 2010). Davis is the creator of a multi-lingual cartoon strip found in seven countries, five languages, and three continents entitled *Besos . . . Kisses . . . Baisers . . . поцелуи.*

Sion Dayson is an American writer living in Paris, France. Her work has appeared in the *Wall Street Journal*, the *Chapel Hill News*, and a National Book

Foundation anthology, among other venues. In 2007 she won a Barbara Deming Award for her fiction. She is currently finishing her MFA degree in writing at the Vermont College of Fine Arts. She explores the Paris that guidebooks don't cover at www.parisimperfect.com.

David Eso is the author of *Entries from My Affair with an Escape Artist* (2004) and founder of the Rocky Mountain literary collective, Migratory Words, which publishes annual anthologies under the same moniker. A career working with special needs children has softened his poetic stylings, and extensive travelling has re-sharpened it at the edges. He has lived and written in France, Syria, Estonia, and Senegal. He is currently tied up in a closet somewhere in Canmore, Alberta (cash reward upon his location).

Megan Fernandes is a PhD student at the University of California, Santa Barbara. She is currently writing a dissertation on cognitive approaches to twentieth-century Irish and American literature. During her time in Paris, she has conducted research at the Center for Literature and Cognition at the Université Paris VIII, and she was published in the latest issue of *Upstairs at Duroc* (2011). She has a forthcoming essay on Beckett to be published in the literary journal, *Miranda* (University Press of Toulouse).

Jorie Graham was born in New York City in 1950. She was raised in Rome, Italy, and educated in French schools. She studied philosophy at the Sorbonne in Paris before attending New York University as an undergraduate, where she studied filmmaking. She received an MFA in poetry from the University of Iowa. Graham is the author of numerous collections of poetry, most recently *Sea Change* (Ecco, 2008), *Never* (2002), *Swarm* (2000), and *The Dream of the Unified Field: Selected Poems 1974-1994*, which won the 1996 Pulitzer Prize for Poetry. Graham has also edited two anthologies, *Earth Took of Earth: 100 Great Poems of* *the English Language* (1996) and *The Best American Poetry 1990*. Her many honours include a John D. and Catherine T. MacArthur Fellowship and the Morton Dauwen Zabel Award from The American Academy and Institute of Arts and Letters. She has taught at the University of Iowa Writers' Workshop and is currently the Boylston Professor of Rhetoric and Oratory at Harvard University. She served as a Chancellor of the Academy of American Poets from 1997 to 2003.

Jeffrey Greene is a graduate of the Iowa Writer's Workshop (MFA) and the University of Houston (PhD). He is the author of four collections of poems. His memoir *French Spirits* (HarperCollins/Bantam) has appeared, to date, in eight countries, and he has written two personalized nature books: *The Golden-Bristled Boar* (forthcoming 2010) and *Water From Stone*. His work has been supported by the National Endowment for the Arts, the Connecticut Commission on the Arts, and the Rinehart Foundation, and he received the Randall Jarrell Award, Discovery/The Nation Award, and Samuel French Morse Prize. His writing has appeared in *The New Yorker, Poetry, The Nation, Ploughshares*, and many other periodicals. After teaching at the University of Houston, University of New Haven, and Goddard MFA, he currently teaches at the American University in Paris.

Jonathan Hamrick was born in Texas and now lives in Los Angeles. He's a PhD student at the University of Southern California. He was in Paris from September 2009 to Bastille Day 2010, working on his dissertation.

Isabel Harding is a fiction writer hailing from Atlanta, Georgia. She graduated from Agnes Scott College in 2009. She spent the following year teaching in Paris and writing stories like "Zombie Mermaid," in a glorified closet of a studio apartment.

Marty Hiatt was born in Melbourne in 1983. He prefers self-directed study to career development. He spent 2010 in Paris, working on a novel and not working on a novel, and doesn't want to leave.

Margaret J. Hults has been the editor, creative co-director, and marketing vice-president of Davis Studios for the past ten years. A writer, musician, and avid history buff, her works include a travelling exhibition titled, *Ten Great State Women*; a radio show, *Sphinx of the Bluegrass*; and *A Peep Show of Women's History*. Previously, she had a career in social services, working with the issues of domestic violence and homelessness in New York City and San Francisco.

Andrea Jonsson grew up in Bozeman, Montana, in a Swedish-American family, playing the violin, hiking, skiing, and writing. She attended McGill University in Montreal, Canada, and received a degree in music performance in 2004 after which she moved to Paris for four years. After writing, reading, teaching, and playing music in Paris, she decided to return to the United States to pursue graduate school in literature. She is currently working towards her PhD in French literature at the University of Pittsburgh.

Julie Kleinman has been writing, teaching, and translating in Paris since 2004. After completing a Master's degree in Social Anthropology at the École des hautes études en sciences sociales in 2007, she returned to her hometown of Boston to begin a PhD in the same field, which happily involved two years of on-site Parisian research. Her translation of *La Politique de la Survie* by Marc Abélès was published by Duke University Press in 2010, and her article on Paris's Gare du Nord will be featured in the *Ethnologie française* journal. In addition to writing her dissertation, she is currently working on her first novel, which takes place in Paris, southern France, and Senegal.

Antonia Klimenko was trained as an actress at the American Conservatory Theatre and has worked briefly in radio, stage, and film. She was first introduced to the literary world on the BBC by the legendary Tambimuttu of Poetry London, who edited and published the likes of Dylan Thomas, T.S. Eliot, Allen Ginsberg, and Leonard Cohen—to name a few. She is a former champion of the San Francisco Poetry Slam and a current "regular" at Spoken Word in Paris.

Sam Langer was born in February 1983 and then finished a BA in May 2007. Now he works casually for Spotless Services at the Alfred Hospital in Melbourne (Australia). His poems have appeared in *Cordite*, *The Age* (Melbourne), *Otoliths*, *Overland*, *Arena*, *The Sun Herald* (Sydney) and *543*, a free poetry magazine he edits and publishes irregularly.

Colin Joseph Wolfgang Mahar was born in New York City. Raised in Montreal, he graduated from McGill University. He later studied at the New College of California in San Francisco, where he earned his Master of Fine Arts in Poetry and Poetics. He currently lives and works in Paris as a teacher, translator, singer/songwriter and, in his better moments—poet.

Alexander Kolya Maksik lived in Paris for seven years before returning to the United States where he's presently a Truman Capote fellow at the Iowa Writers' Workshop. In Paris he taught literature, worked as a translator, a journalist, and a guidebook writer. His first novel, *You Deserve Nothing*, will be published in September by Tonga Books. His short stories, essays, and poems have been published in France, the UK, the United States, the United Arab Emirates and the Czech Republic. His work has appeared or is forthcoming in *nthposition*, *nthWORD*, *The Texas Observer*, *Above Magazine*, *Crate*, *Upstairs at Duroc*, and the *Nervous Breakdown* where he's a regular contributor.

Jessica Malcomson spent a year in Paris before returning to the UK to study in London. Sadly, she died shortly before publication of this anthology. She was a promising young writer and a friend. We miss her and her Cheshire Cat grin.

Danielle McShine was born in Trinidad and Tobago. She has lived in Venezuela and in the US, where she studied music and French linguistics. Her poems have appeared in *The Adirondack Review, Thunder Sandwich*, and other online magazines. She lives in France.

Alice Notley was born in Bisbee, Arizona, on November 8, 1945 and grew up in Needles, California, in the Mojave Desert. She was educated at Barnard College and at the Writers' Workshop, University of Iowa. During the late sixties and early seventies she lived a travelling poet's life (San Francisco, Bolinas, London, Wivenhoe, Chicago) before settling on New York's Lower East Side. For sixteen years, she was an important force in the eclectic second generation of the so-called New York School of poetry. Notley, who now lives in Paris, is the author of more than thirty books of poetry, including *At Night the States*, the double volume *Close to Me and Closer . . . (The Language of Heaven)* and *Désamère*, and *How Spring Comes*, which was a co-winner of the San Francisco Poetry Award. Her epic poem *The Descent of Alette* was published by Penguin in 1996, followed by *Mysteries of Small Houses* (1998), which was one of three finalists for the Pulitzer Prize and the winner of the *Los Angeles Times* Book Prize for Poetry. Notley's long poem *Disobedience* won the Griffin Poetry Prize in 2002. In 2005 the University of Michigan Press published her book of essays on poetry, *Coming After*. Notley recently edited *The Collected Poems of Ted Berrigan* (University of California Press), with her sons Anselm Berrigan and Edmund Berrigan as co-editors. Her most recent books are *Alma, or The Dead Women*, from Granary Books; *Grave of Light: New and Selected Poems*, from Wesleyan, and winner of the Academy of American Poets' Lenore Marshall Award; and *In the Pines*, from Penguin. Forthcoming in 2011 is *Culture of One*.

Helen Cusack O'Keeffe has lived in Paris since 2008, but has visited the city as much as she can for most of her life. She discovered the joys of Russian literature whilst in the throes of her first degree, and also spent time in Moscow, St. Petersburg, and Siberia as part of her studies. She later pursued an MA as a social worker, her area of research interest being bereavement. After qualifying she worked for several years in a mental health service for homeless people in London. This extract comes from her first novel, *Bittern's Last Folly*, the final draft of which is in progress.

Lisa Pasold has been thrown off a train in Belarus, been cheated in the Venetian gambling halls of Ca' Vendramin Calergi, and mushed huskies in the Yukon. She has published two books of poetry, *Weave* and *A Bad Year for Journalists*, as well as a novel, *Rats of Las Vegas*. Lisa grew up in Montreal, which gave her the necessary jaywalking skills to survive in Paris.

Rufo Quintavalle was born in London in 1978, studied at Oxford and the University of Iowa, and now lives in Paris. He is the author of a chapbook, *Make Nothing Happen* (Oystercatcher Press, 2009) and is widely published in print and online journals. He helps edit the literary magazine, *Upstairs at Duroc*, and is currently acting poetry editor for the award-winning webzine, *nthposition*.

Alberto Rigettini is an Italian playwright and screenwriter. He is the host of Spoken Word Paris and a member of the poetic sect of the Megalomaniacs. His poems presented in this collection are excerpts from a book he is currently writing in four languages about five countries: England, France ("When you sleep and your flower reposes"), Italy, Spain ("Last bath in Malaga"), and the

United States. In recent years, he has read at the Bowery Poetry Club in New York City and won a screenwriting competition at the Bay One-Acts Festival in San Francisco for his play, *The Sentimental Boxer*.

Sarah Riggs is a poet, translator, and visual artist. She is the author of *Waterwork* (Chax Press, 2007) and *Chain of Miniscule Decisions in the Form of a Feeling* (Reality Street Editions, 2007). *60 Textos* (Ugly Duckling Presse, 2010), along with *28 télégrammes* and *43 Post-Its* were first published in France (éditions de l'Attente, translated by Françoise Valéry, 2006–09). Riggs has also published a book of essays, *Word Sightings: Poetry and Visual Media in Stevens, Bishop, and O'Hara* (Routledge, 2002). After producing the Tangier 8 cinépoèmes in Morocco in 2009, she is currently working on a film poem based on Virginia Woolf. A member of the bilingual poetry association Double Change, www. doublechange.org, and director of Tamaas, www.tamaas.org, an international multicultural nonprofit, Riggs currently teaches at NYU-in-France.

Eleni Sikelianos is the author of a hybrid memoir (*The Book of Jon*) and six books of poetry, the most recent being *Body Clock*. She has been the happy recipient of various awards for her poetry, nonfiction, and translations, and her work has been translated into a dozen languages. One volume has appeared in French and two more (*The Book of Jon* and *The California Poem*) will appear in France next year. She has translated *Exchanges on Light* by Jacques Roubaud and is spending her current sabbatical in Paris.

Kathleen Spivack is the author of *A History of Yearning*, 2010, the winner of the Sow's Ear International Poetry Chapbook Prize. She also won a First Prize, the Allen Ginsberg Poetry Award, the Mumford Prize, and several Best Travel Essay awards, 2010. Author of six previous books of prose and poetry (Doubleday, Graywolf, Earthwinds/Grolier, etc.) and Pulitzer nominee, her work appears in numerous magazines and anthologies. Fellowships include Radcliffe Institute, NEA, Howard, Mass Council, Fulbright, Yaddo, MacDowell, and others. With Robert Lowell, a personal memoir, with portraits of Bishop, Sexton, Plath, Kunitz, and others of her time, is forthcoming from the University Press of New England, 2011. Kathleen Spivack teaches in Paris and Boston.

Cole Swensen has published twelve volumes of poetry and has received various awards, including the Iowa Poetry Prize, the SF State Poetry Center Book Award, a National Poetry Series, and a Guggenheim Fellowship. She is also a translator of French poetry, prose, and art criticism, and runs the small press La Presse. Her collected essays are coming out next year from the University of Michigan Press.

Elizabeth Willis is the author of five books of poetry: *Address* (Wesleyan, 2011); *Meteoric Flowers* (Wesleyan, 2006); *Turneresque* (Burning Deck, 2003); *The Human Abstract* (Penguin, 1995); and *Second Law* (Avenue B, 1993). A collective translation begun at cipM in 2007 resulted in the publication of *Fleurs Météoriques* (cipM/Un bureau sur l'Atlantique, 2009). *Loi Deux*, translated by Juliette Valéry, was published by Format Américain in 1994. Other translations into French have appeared in *Texte, Action Poetique, Doublechange, Arsenal,* and *Walt Whitman Hom(m)age.*

Neil Uzzell is a twenty-seven-year-old American from North Carolina who doesn't like to talk about himself in the third person. He is getting his MFA in fiction writing at California College of the Arts in San Francisco. He teaches part-time, works on the school's literary journal, and likes to play honky-tonk blues on his guitar. He lived in France from 2005 to 2008. If you would like to read more work by Neil, you can find him on Facebook.

A GUIDE TO THE
LITERARY SCENE IN PARIS

Writer Jen K. Dick's comprehensive monthly listing of literary events and readings in Paris: fragment78 (http://parisreadingsmonthlylisting.blogspot.com)

Poetry reading series:

- SpokenWord Paris (http://spokenwordparis.blogspot.com), an open mike run by David Barnes
- Ivy Writers Paris, run by writers Jen K. Dick and Michelle Noteboom (http://ivywritersparis.blogspot.com)
- Double Change, bilingual online journal and reading series organized by Vincent Broqua and Olivier Brossard (http://www.doublechange.com)
- Poets Live reading series featuring published (English-language) poets, organized by Dylan Harris (http://poets-live.com)
- WICE and *Upstairs at Duroc*: WICE runs writing courses featuring such writers as Alice Notley, publishes the journal *Upstairs at Duroc*, and puts on readings (http://www.wice-paris.org/)

About expat writing in Paris:

- *Ekleksographia*, a poetry magazine with an issue devoted to France (http://ekleksographia.ahadadabooks.com/france/index.html)
- Laurel Zuckerman, a Franco-American writer who blogs about the expat writing scene in Paris (http://www.laurelzuckerman.com/paris-writer-news)

Exciting online magazines with a Paris connection:

- *Nthposition* (http://www.nthposition.com)
- *Versal* (http://www.wordsinhere.com)